THE
JOURNEY
THE BEAST BOOK 1

KATHERINE HELENE

authorHOUSE®

AuthorHouse™
1663 Liberty Drive
Bloomington, IN 47403
www.authorhouse.com
Phone: 1-800 839-8640

Published by AuthorHouse 11/18/2013

ISBN: 978-1-4918-3192-2 (sc)
ISBN: 978-1-4918-3191-5 (e)

Library of Congress Control Number: 2013919672

For William Caulton

Contents

CHAPTER 1

ANA

THE SUN WAS sinking below the trees casting a glow over the forest. The trees that were still alive were almost bare. The buds were beginning to grow as a sign that spring was almost there. The March wind ripped through my thin coat. As I lay under an old oak tree, I listened silently for sounds of movement. I feared my stomach would grumble and scare off all the game, so I chewed on a mint leaf to tame my hunger. It had been a few days since my twin brother Logan brought home a rabbit. He was out hunting on the other side of our little forest.

Our forest used to spread out for miles behind our cozy house. I remember when I was little how my father would put me on his shoulders while Logan walked beside us into our forest. He would point out different trees and plants and make us sit down and be silent so we could hear the sounds of the forest. The birds would chirp and the deer would chew on leaves and let us be. We didn't disturb them and they trusted us. My mom would join us sometimes; rather than plants she knew about the birds and the squirrels and the quiet animals hiding all around us. After we returned, mom always had a steaming bowl of soup ready for us. We would walk in the house, our cheeks rosy and our hands cold even though Mom made sure we wore mittens, but we were happy.

When I was little, I didn't know what hunger was. It was the small grumble from my stomach that a piece of one of mom's homemade loafs of bread could fix and then I could finish exploring. I grew up on three meals a day with snacks in between. I could splurge on ice cream or take an extra scoop of mashed potatoes.

What I would have given for three meals a day.

A crunch in the leaves snapped me back to reality. I held my bow at the ready and waited for another sound. There is a crunch behind me and I turn around to find Logan holding a small excuse of a squirrel. "You are never going to catch anything unless you at least attempt to conceal yourself."

I glanced around and realized he was probably right. Rather than crouching next to a tree I could have at least made a blind inside of a bush or under some low-hanging branches.

"Got anything?" he asked. I shook my head no so he trudged off in the direction of our house. I followed silently behind him.

Logan is my twin brother, although we don't look much alike. He is taller than me by a few inches and he has lighter hair than I do. Even his facial features are much stronger than mine. While he has a defined jaw line and prominent features mine are much more rounded and soft, almost baby-like. It made me look timid and weak while he looks strong and determined. It was a trait I had always been jealous of.

Logan skinned the squirrel while I made up a fire. Soon the logs were burning and Logan had the squirrel stabbed with a stick. He used another stick as a fork in the ground and rested the squirrel over the fire to cook. It tasted delicious in my mouth but was too soon gone. My few lousy bites did almost nothing to diminish my hunger, but I didn't say anything. I owed Logan because he caught our last two meals while I hadn't seen anything.

After dinner we picked ourselves up and headed inside. We lived in a small white house, one floor, three bedrooms, a living room, bathroom and what's left of a kitchen. Two months before our stove caught on fire while Logan tried to cook a turkey he shot. All that's left were two cabinets that were stocked with old cans. They quickly diminished over the next six months and with no real town anymore there was no way for us to get food except for our forest.

Our town used to be beautiful. Valparaiso had a movie theater, shopping centers, and teen centers, even an Oberweis ice cream shop!

Our school was filled with all of the cliché cliques and normal days of grabbing coffee beforehand and ditching lasts period. But I hadn't been to school in a year. No one had.

Last year was when everything collapsed. June 2098. Our town, our state, our government. What happened? World War III happened. It started with Asia and quickly spread throughout the Middle East. They started by bombing in Europe. The United States second. The capital was the first to go. Without a government, the country was severely weakened. They sent bombs to New York, California, Nevada, Florida, Colorado, and Illinois. Unfortunately, Valparaiso was only sixty-five miles from where the bomb landed in Illinois. It easily wiped out everything within a fifty mile radius of it, and it affected everything else fifty more miles outside of ground zero. The United States population was diminished to about eighty million people.

People who survived the bomb fled to their capital cities. They were searching for rescue camps and shelters, food, and just to get away from the catastrophe. Did they ever find it? I didn't know. My parents, Logan, and I survived and we scavenged the vacant houses around us for canned goods or anything else we could eat. Together we survived. Dad and Logan usually went out to hunt while Mom and I scavenged the town.

We lasted six months. Then one morning, Logan shook me awake yelling about not being able to find mom or dad. We spent the next week searching the town; nothing. I don't know where they went or why, only that they abandoned us.

And for that, they will never be forgiven.

My parents were scientists. They worked for a science lab just outside of town. They never wanted to talk about work. Logan and I tried many times to get them to open up about what they do at work and why they love it. All we got was, "It's confidential," and, "sometimes life has a plan for you that you didn't expect." Logan and I tried to figure out what they meant by that, but all we could think of was they hadn't expected to love science and much as they did.

The day Mom and Dad disappeared was just another normal day. Mom took me out to search through more neighbors' houses while Dad and Logan went out hunting. We found a can of corn and a blanket. Most of the houses had already been thoroughly searched. We came back home at the end of the day with Logan and Dad cooking a rabbit and a small bird they had found. I had wanted the rabbit but kept my mouth shut when Dad handed me half of the bird. Logan was given the other half, so I couldn't be too upset. I scarfed down the scrawny bits of meat which only seemed to cause my stomach to crave more rather than satisfy it.

After eating we played a game we came up with called "Who Survived." It's like charades, but you can only be people. You get one word to describe yourself and then you act out a famous person. If one of us guesses the person, they survived. If we didn't guess right, they didn't survive. Pretty simple, but it was one of the things I looked forward to each day.

I remember being tired during "Who Survived" that night. I was lying on the ground. Logan seemed pretty worn out too, although he was laughing and participating in the game a lot more than I was. I fell asleep during the game. The last thing I remember was Dad acting out a crazy person. I couldn't decipher his actions. They were wild and sporadic and he even left the room multiple times and I think he locked the windows. Although Dad had always been a decent actor, there was something about him that seemed over exuberant. His eyes, they were all too alive, but I just can't recall the details from that night like I should be able to.

When I caught myself contemplating his actions I pushed the thoughts out of my mind. I didn't like to remember my parents after they abandoned us.

How much corn?" Logan asked.

"Um, eight cans," I answered. We were stocking inventory.

"Peas?"

"Two."

"Do we have any tomato soup left?"

"One can."

"How about green beans?" Logan asked.

"Two more cans."

"Is there anything else?"

"No," I answered. I closed the cabinet drawer. Only thirteen cans of food left. I looked at Logan. He stared right back at me. He let out a deep sigh and rubbed his hand over his face. After a minute he brought his hand down, shook his head in hopeless defeat, and left me alone in the kitchen.

CHAPTER 2

CARTER

"WHERE IS MY crutch?" I thought aloud to myself. I raised myself up off the couch and scanned the room. It was lying mostly under the couch, a tiny end sticking out for me to find. I dropped to my left knee and reached for it. The pain in my right leg was intense. When I stood back up, I leaned heavily on my crutch to examine it.

There was a long scar reaching from my shin to my thigh. The swelling had gone down increasingly, but it was still raw and abhorrent. I limped to the bathroom and pulled out my tube of antibiotic cream. I rolled up the end and pushed out the last bit of cream. I smeared it onto my leg and sighed. I was officially out of antibiotic cream and now the wound would have to finish healing on its own.

I hobbled to the kitchen and opened the last can of corn from my counter. I grabbed a fork out of the sink of dishes I had cleaned the night before and walked back into the living room to eat. I hadn't been able to hunt because of my leg, and over the last few weeks my food stash dwindled down to the can of corn in my hands and some canned beans.

As I leaned back on the couch and enjoyed my cold corn, I thought about what had happened. I thought about the night my dad disappeared, and the night I was attacked. The thoughts perpetually haunted me and I tried to push them out of my mind.

Before WWIII I would watch TV and play video games to get my mind off things. Now, I could read or hunt. Usually I chose hunting. Reading never interested me. It took too long. I liked watching movies because they tell a whole story in two hours.

I finished my corn and threw it out with window into the Able Disposal garbage can, where that tin can will stay for a long time. I hadn't taken out the trash in months. I had hardly any trash these days—only the few cans I eat each week, if any—and considering there was no garbage company to come pick up my garbage, I didn't see the need to take it out.

I groaned and hobbled to the bathroom. I rummaged through the medicine cabinet and found an old ace bandage. I wrapped it around my leg, but it only covered my shin and knee. I searched for another ace bandage to support my thigh, but couldn't find one. I ended up taking an old t-shirt out of my dad's closet and securing it with clothes pins and duct tape I found lying in a pile on his dresser.

I headed to my room and on the way stopped in the hall closet and pulled out my dark green back pack. I sat on my bed and unpacked it. I had added emergency supplies once we started hearing warning sirens and having blackout practices in case the United States was bombed. I pulled out a tin water bottle that could be strapped onto my belt, a flash light with an extra set of batteries, and an emergency medical box I made in grade school for a project in my boy scout troop.

And people laugh at boy scouts.

Inside the medical box were Band-Aids, a small tube of toothpaste and a miniature toothbrush, a gauze pad, and what's left of a miniature-sized tube of antibiotic cream. Unfortunately, there wasn't enough cream for my entire leg and there wasn't an ace bandage. I decided to fill the box with the rest of the Band Aids from the medicine cabinet, and the poison ivy spray. There was only half a bottle left, but it could come in handy.

I opened my closet doors to see if I had any clean clothes left. I hate to admit it but I hadn't exactly kept up with my laundry because I was too lazy to boil water and scrub my clothes when I needed to be hunting and resting my leg. I found two stray t-shirts and two pairs of jeans that weren't too bad. Then I grabbed my only sweatshirt, a grey sweatshirt that said Bowling Green on it in orange letters. I bought it when my school was traveling around looking at colleges. My favorite had been Bowling Green State University in Ohio.

I had just one pair of tennis shoes left; my other pair was destroyed in an incident I didn't want to relive. I wore the old, faded blue Nike's and looked around my room. I decided to pack a few extra pairs of socks and boxers and zipped up my backpack. On my way out of my bedroom I grabbed my black sleeping bad and tied it onto my backpack. Upon exiting for the second time, I stopped, turned around, and in a small chest on my desk I pulled out a bottle of scotch and threw it in.

I made my way into the kitchen and pulled out all of my can goods. I had scavenged many cans from the houses of neighbors who had fled, but my stash had dwindled down to ten cans. It hadn't been easy changing my eating habits, so the first month I devoured more cans than the last five months put together. Before I was used to three meals a day. After I was lucky with one meal a day. I never let myself eat more than four cans a week so I could stay here longer. I hunted most of the days in the second month of what I call The Ending. I referred to the time after the war when the world finally decided it would be coming to an end as The Ending. Everyone knew it wouldn't last much longer. We survived 2000, 2012, and 2051, but the people of 2099 aren't going to live to see 2100.

At least that's my prediction.

After the accident though, I hadn't been able to hunt much especially during my first few weeks of recovery. I could barely walk. That's why I made my cane. I still had to use it months later, but my leg was almost healed.

I couldn't afford to stay at my house much longer. I had to leave Wanatah, Indiana. As much as I loved it there, I had to face the fact that my dad wasn't coming back, I was running out of food, and my leg was healing. I could hunt again and I needed to find another place to live.

I grabbed my dad's hand gun along with its shells and threw them into my backpack. Then I grabbed his hunting bow and set of arrows, closed the door, looked left and right even though there was no need, and crossed the street.

CHAPTER 3

ANA

"**H**AVE YOU EVER seen anything like this before?" I asked Logan somberly. We were walking through the main mall strips of Valparaiso and everything was destroyed. The Super Target's windows were shattered, the doors jammed open with shopping carts. There were a few stray cars in the parking lot that were all practically destroyed. Logan and I had searched the town for a car to drive around so we could search other neighboring towns, but every car was either out of gas or so demolished it would never run.

With so little of anything left in the house, Logan suggested we search around all the strip malls downtown for anything that could be useful. It was a false hope but one we couldn't simply pass up. Besides, I was looking forward to finding some new books at the old Barnes and Noble that had been here for over one hundred years. It was my favorite store, but I was openly disappointed when we got nearer to the store.

Like the Target, the windows were smashed as were the glass doors. We stepped through the door frame and into the building. There was almost nothing. The only book I saw was a Dictionary and even the book shelves had been ripped apart. Most of the wooden book shelves were gone; people probably used them for firewood.

"I'm sorry, Ana," Logan told me.

I just nodded my head. I didn't need to cry, but my spirits were crushed for the rest of the day. We walked through Lowes, Best Buy, Office Max, and we even tried McDonalds looking for an abandoned sack of potatoes. The only thing Logan and I found even remotely useful was in Menards. A tin bucket that was dented and not even close to being round anymore became our possession. The handle was only connected to it on one side but Logan said we could repair it and the bucket would be good as new.

Yeah right. I didn't tell Logan this though, because there was always the small chance it would actually come in handy.

The March wind numbed our noses as we trudged the two miles back home. It was a wasted day that only caused our hunger levels to rise. My fingers were freezing; the temperature was about 40 degrees though so I didn't think they were frost bitten. I was hoping to find another pair of gloves today, but even before we left that morning I knew I probably wouldn't.

When we reached home the first thing Logan and I did was haul the rest of the chopped wood inside. This took about five trips each and when it was finished Logan decided to go cut more. He instructed me to start and fire and once it was going to come help him bring in the wood he chopped.

Pretty soon I had a fire going and I groaned before I stepped outside so Logan wouldn't hear me. I despised carrying wood inside even though he needed my help. Logan did a lot of hard work so I needed to make sure I did my fair share as well.

After six trips to and from the house with my arms loaded with wood, I grabbed my bow and arrows and set off to hunt. By some miracle I got lucky. I set a trap and only an hour later I heard the *click!* of the snare. I looked around from my spot on the ground to see if there was any more wild life with in shooting range, but there wasn't. I ventured over to the snare and found that I had managed to snag a rabbit. It wasn't entirely too small and I trudged back to the house with a grin on my face.

Logan noticed my change in mood as I cleaned the rabbit and he decided to get out his guitar. He hardly ever played his guitar anymore, but tonight he played my favorite song. There weren't lyrics, just a melody he had written, but it made my evening. He strummed the familiar chords and for a few minutes, life wasn't so bad. If my stomach hadn't been trying to claw its way out of me, it would have been truly enjoyable.

"I miss you playing," I confessed to Logan.

"I sort of do too," he agreed. He sighed and set down the guitar.

"Don't stop playing," I asked. "I love the sound of your guitar. It's one of the only happy things left."

Logan lifted back up his guitar and played another song. He strummed and I sang a few versus. Together we sounded not too bad. I fell asleep that night on our old couch in front of the fire with Logan in our Lazy Boy chair with his guitar still resting in his lap.

CHAPTER 4

CARTER

THE STREET STRETCHED on endlessly into the setting sun. It's a blazing ball of orange streaking out into the surrounding sky. I'd been traveling down this single road for a week. I used three of my canned food and tomorrow I'd have to leave the road and head into the first woods I found. I needed to hunt. I couldn't rely on my canned food and my bundle was diminishing fast.

It was eerily quiet. There were no howls, no chirps of birds or cooing of owls. There wasn't even the scurry sounds of squirrels traveling from branch to branch in the trees above. At the beginning of The Ending, the quietness terrified me. I used to think something was waiting in the Quiet; that it would jump out when I had my back turned. I wanted to sleep with my lights on every night, but there was no electricity. I wouldn't ever sleep. I would stay awake out of fright and pull the covers up to my eyes for protection. It was like living in a horror movie.

It got better as time went on. I probably wasted ten batteries in my flashlight that I kept on all night pointed at my bedroom door. Eventually I became used to The Quiet and turned off my flashlight. I always kept it next to me though. I also started sleeping on the couch after the Incident, and when winter hit because I needed the fireplace to stay warm.

When the sun finally sunk below the horizon completely and the moon started shining, I turned off the road. I found a giant oak tree a few yards inward and untied my sleeping bag. There were giant roots sticking out from the tree forming a little alcove and I squeezed my sleeping bag inside and try to stay warm.

The first night I thought about climbing a tree to stay out of danger's reach, but I found it to be disastrous. The good branches to sleep in were too high up to support my weight. I was only 125 pounds, but the added weight of my backpack was too much.

So far I liked sleeping on the ground. I hadn't had any problems with snakes or spiders, or any animal for that matter. Besides, when I slept on the ground I found I could look up and stare at the stars that shine bright. They were a promise that the days would get better as long as they could still shine.

I spent the entire next day hunting. I finally found a small bird and almost missed it. I had to use my hand gun to shoot it because it was too small for an arrow. My stomach begged me to open my last can of corn or to hunt again, but I knew I couldn't. If I started walking I could focus on the road ahead of me and I could forget about my hunger. All the towns I had passed through had been completely deserted. Everyone must have been heading south to Indianapolis.

This didn't put a damper on my spirits though. I didn't think they could get much better or worse. My spirits were somewhere in the middle of caring and being too tired to care. I got through each day trying to stay warm and find something to eat. If anything even remotely interesting happened, it was not happening to me.

I decided to head somewhat north and see if there were any other survivors closer to Chicago. Eventually I'd have to move along, but I didn't want to go all the way to Indianapolis. I figured I might as well check out Northwest Indiana. I could stop at the bigger cities, more urban populated areas besides Gary. I didn't plan on stopping there.

I strapped my rolled-up sleeping bag onto my backpack, slung it over my shoulders, and stepped back onto the road. I had a few hours of daylight left to travel before the sun set. I was only a few miles from the outskirts of Valparaiso, so my goal was to be there by nightfall.

When I entered the tiny woods on the very border of Valparaiso, the first thing I saw in the darkness was a light. I maneuvered through the trees and bushes and climbed over a few fallen trees to see that the light is a fire. It's inside a small white house and sleeping near the fire were two people.

CHAPTER 5

ANA

I WOKE TO THE sound of the fire popping. I opened my heavy eyelids to see Logan loading another log onto the fire. I looked at the window and saw it was still dark out.

"What time is it?" I asked him.

Logan looked at his watch. "Just after three."

His watch was on its last set of batteries and once they died, we would be relying on purely the sun for any sense of time.

"Go back to sleep," Logan instructed me. It wasn't hard. By the time he was finished speaking, my eyelids felt like they were being weighed down and I was out.

The next time I opened my eyes the sun was streaming through the window warming my face. I heard Logan in the back of the house rummaging through some boxes. We packed all of mom and dad's stuff away when they left because it was taking up pointless space. I wrapped the throw blanket around my shoulders and trudged off to see what Logan was looking for.

I found his up to his neck in cardboard boxes. "Um, what are you doing, Logan?"

He jumped, and knocked over two of the boxes.

"Sorry!" I apologized and picked up the boxes and placed them back on top of their piles.

"You scared me half to death!" Logan laughed.

"What are you looking for?" I asked again.

"Didn't we put away all of Dad's prize hunting guns?"

"Yeah. We aren't supposed to touch them."

"Yeah, well I think that rule is over," Logan argued.

I paused. "Dad isn't ever coming back, is he?"

Logan sighed and shook his head. "I don't think so, Ana."

We stood looking around at the boxes. "Will you help me find them?" Logan asked. I nodded my head yes and folded my blanket in a pile on the floor by the doorway and picked up a box.

"I've already sorted through those already. Could you start on that side?" Logan asked.

"Oops!" I closed the box and grabbed a new box on a pile on the other side of the room. We sorted through every single box and didn't find any of Dad's hunting guns. "Where could they be?" I asked.

Logan pondered the thought then slapped his forehead. "I can't believe I forgot! I put them in the garage!" He jumped up and ran out of the room. I let out a breath of exasperation, picked up my blanket, and headed out to the garage. There was Logan pulling out all three of Dad's guns and ten boxes of bullets.

"I can't believe we wasted an hour in that room when they were in the first box you opened out here!" I laughed then went back inside the house where I loaded another log on the fire and opened up a can of green beans.

While I was cooking those, Logan walked in the living room with one of Dad's guns. "I'm going out to the woods. It looks like it might rain so this could be our last chance to hunt for tomorrow unless you feel like getting drenched and catching a cold. Plus I don't have anything else to do." He smiled one of his rare smiles and closed the door behind him.

I ate half of the green beans out of the can and put the can next to the fire so it would stay warm for Logan to eat when he comes back later tonight. I threw another log on the small fire to keep it going for another hour and noticed the pile was getting smaller. If it was going to rain tomorrow it would be a bad time to chop wood. I sighed and put on my coat and Logan's thick gloves.

I found the logs Logan had chopped away from the tree he cut down and I picked one up and put it on the tree stump. I set the ax on the top of the log and carefully aimed where I was going to whack the log. I raised the ax and brought it down with all my might. The ax went part of the way into the log and got stuck. I lifted the log onto the ground and stepped on it to pull the ax out. I placed it back on the tree stump, took a deep breath and swung again.

The log didn't quite break. Instead the ax was stuck in the wood and no matter how hard I pulled it wouldn't budge. So with the log still on the end of the ax I swung a third time and brought it down hard, finally snapping the log in two. I pushed the pieces onto the ground and picked up another log. By the time I chopped three logs down, I was out of breath and my arm was so sore I could barely hold the ax.

I carried the ax along with three pieces of wood into the house and then returned to the stump to retrieve the other pieces. I picked them up and when I turned to head inside I tripped over one of the tree roots from the stump and dropped two logs. I tried to bend down and pick up the logs and one of the logs in my hand fell out and onto the ground. I let out a small screech of exasperation and when I reached out again for the logs, a hand beat me there.

I looked up and saw Logan holding a rabbit and carrying the two extra logs I couldn't manage. I grabbed the last log on the ground and we headed inside together. "Thanks!" I said. "I almost lost it there for a second!"

He chuckled. "You shouldn't have been cutting the wood, Ana."

"I know but tomorrow if it rains we won't be able to cut anymore and the pile inside will get low again."

"It gets low every day."

With a heavy sigh Ana agreed. "At least it'll be summer soon and then we will only need fires when we eat."

Logan opened the door and dropped his wood on the fire. He set to work skinning the rabbit and setting the meat to cook.

"That can of beans is yours too," I said as I placed the wood in my arms on the pile.

"Thanks, Ana."

Logan was very quiet while he was cooking the rabbit. I knew something was wrong. "Logan? Is something bothering you?"

He waited a moment looking for the right answer. "Yeah. I'm not sure how to say this." He started. I sat down on the couch and waited patiently. "I don't know how much longer we can stay here," he blurted out. "I was lucky today with this rabbit, but it's not going to be this way for long. Our cans are running too low and the animals are too scarce." He looked at me with seriousness in his eyes I hadn't seen there before.

"Ana, pack your bags tonight. We are leaving in the morning."

CHAPTER 6

CARTER

I SLOWLY OPENED MY eyes. The sound of footsteps roused me and instantly I was wide awake. I rolled up my sleeping bag and shoved it along with my backpack in the bush next to me. I quickly dove on top on my bag and hid. I'd been hiding in the woods behind the white house for two weeks now. The boy and the girl hadn't noticed me yet, thankfully. The girl and boy both seemed around my age, maybe a year younger than me. I was seventeen and the boy might be the same age, but the girl seemed too small and fragile to be seventeen.

It was the boy this time who exited the house. He'd been bringing out really nice guns. I wished I could get the chance to see what kind they were. The girl always just brought a bow. From what I could tell it was very intricate and detailed. I'd have liked to get the chance to inspect that bow up close too.

Thankfully the boy walked a few yards past me and then turned to venture deeper into the woods to look for a good place to hunt. When I couldn't hear his footsteps anymore, I pulled my backpack out from under me and I rolled my sleeping bag up tighter. I relaxed and leaned against the tree. I wouldn't be doing anything today since the boy was hunting. If I had gotten up and wandered away I could have be mistaken for an animal and that would have ended poorly on my part.

These were some of my favorite days because I didn't have to worry about anything. I ended up curling in a ball and going back to sleep. When I heard footsteps that woke me yet again, the sun was high in the sky. It was around two o'clock and when the boy passed by I ducked down and kept quiet. He didn't notice anything different, just walked on towards the house.

Once he was gone I pulled out my own bow and set off in the opposite direction. Sometimes it was better to hunt in the evening. It was more peaceful and usually the boy and girl weren't around. The boy had walked away empty handed, but I ended up getting a small squirrel. I didn't like taking any chances of being spotted, so whenever I got a catch I went to the end of the woods and crossed the empty street. I looked both ways again. It was such a habit.

When I was finished eating, I unwrapped my leg to examine my wound. It was a little inflamed, but not as much as I thought it would be. I pulled my medical kit out of my back pack and squeezed out the very last drops of antibiotic cream. The ace bandage was getting dirty, but it was too late to travel all the way to the river to clean it. I rewrapped my leg and leaned back on the ground.

That night as I looked up at the stars, all I could see were clouds. I could tell it was going to rain the next day, and the last time it rained I got a cold. I didn't want to go through that again.

It was time I met the boy and the girl.

Chapter 7

Beast

BOOM! I snap alert at the sound. I rush to investigate. Smoke. Smoke everywhere. A Voice in my head. A hole in the wall. I'm free.

SNIFF. I sniff all around. New place. New world. New creatures. New smells. Good smells. Good sounds. I trot off into the forest. I go where ever the Voice says to go. I walk a long time.

CRUNCH! I step on sticks. I keep my nose on the ground. Searching. Searching. Where is it? Voice says keep going. Dark. Trees. Bushes. Dead. Alive. Squirrel! I chase squirrel. Voice yells. Turns me around. Stay on path. Not much farther.

I stop. Voice says good. Voice says smell. I smell. I smell again. I found it! The scent is here. I track the scent. I follow it through more trees. More bushes.

House.

CHAPTER 8

ANA

THE SUN ROSE too soon and I sat up. I packed my bag last night so I didn't have to worry about it this morning. Logan and I were leaving. We were heading to Lafayette, then farther south until we reach Indianapolis and found a safe zone. Hopefully there would be places for us to stay on the way.

It was a warm day, almost 75 degrees. I dunked a washcloth in a bucket of water I collected to wipe my arms and legs and face. I threw on my blue Colts t-shirt and a pair of black shorts. I pulled on socks and tied up my old tennis shoes. My hair was a mess that just got thrown into a ponytail, and I pulled my backpack over my shoulders.

I packed all my clothes: five t-shirts, three pairs of shorts, two pairs of jeans, a sweatshirt, a light jacket, and an extra pair of tennis shoes. Two cans of food were in my bag—the other three in Logan's. I had a flashlight that contained the last pair of batteries, a map of Indiana, and my kitchen knife. My sleeping bag was rolled up and secured on top of my back pack.

I turned to say goodbye to the only bedroom of mine I'd ever known. I took a mental picture of the purple walls, wooden dresser and desk, purple polka dot bedspread with my teddy bear resting peacefully on top. Before I closed the door, I took a glance at my bookshelf. It was filled with books, but I knew I couldn't bring them all with me. I run back over and pick up <u>My Sister's Keeper</u>. It was my great grandma's favorite book which she convinced my mom to read. It was mom's favorite book too, so she convinced me to read it and I loved it just as much. I quickly stuffed it in my back pack and left the room. As I closed the door I couldn't help the small tear that escaped.

I quickly wiped it away and wandered into the kitchen. It was then that I noticed how quiet it was. I set my pack down and listened. I didn't hear Logan. He should have been up by now. I walked to the end of the hall and reached his room. His door was ajar so I pushed it open the rest of the way. He wasn't there. *Where could he have gone?* His bed was unmade. His sheets were strewn about the floor. I noticed his backpack was sitting on his desk. I opened it to find it completely packed.

I ventured back down the hallway looking for a clue of where Logan might've gone. I looked in the closet, our parents' room, and nothing. I reached the end of the hall and glanced at the front door. It was wide open which was odd. I inspected the door more closely and realized the screen was gone. The main door was wide open, leaving a hole where the screen ought to have been. I stepped outside without having to open the screen door; I saw a trail in the dirt. The trail was almost continuous. There were small ruts and lines outside the main path. It was as if someone was being dragged along and they were flailing their arms and legs to try and escape. Is this where Logan went? Was he dragging someone—or something—away?

Or was he the one being dragged?

I stopped walking halfway to the woods. I followed the trail with my eyes all the way to the woods. Something was definitely wrong. I could feel it in the pit of my stomach. I returned to the kitchen and inspected the rest of the house. I locked the front door and looked around. Everything else seemed normal and nothing was out of place. I decided to wait out the day for him.

The sun woke me. I sat up off the couch and realized I was still gripping my small pocket knife. I stood up, stretching my stiff muscles and walked around the house. I looked around, but my hopes were quickly deminished. Logan was not back.

I went to Logan's room and pulled out the cans of food from his backpack, his flashlight and compass, and his sweatshirts and stuffed them into my bag. At the very bottom of his backpack, I found a picture of our family. It was taken before everything fell apart. It was taken when the Talley's were just an average American family. When we were happy. When we were together. I pushed the thoughts out of my mind, and slid the picture into my pocket.

I walked through our house one more time, grabbed my bow and arrows, then closed the door and set out into our woods.

The woods surrounded me. They closed in on me, trapped me. The trees loomed above taunting me. I tried to follow the path that was in my yard, but less than fifty paces into the forest it was eaten by the bushes and trees. I stopped after a few hours of wandering around looking for the trail again. I leaned up against a tree and let out a long sigh.

I stared at the trees around me. The little foliage that's left did little to block out the sun. Though the sun was shining bright, April in Indiana could still be cold. I shivered and pulled a sweatshirt out of my back pack. I picked Logan's navy blue sweatshirt, which smelled like him. As I continued walking my stomach grumbled and I realized I was hungry. I thought about opening one of my cans of food. The corn sounded so good. I couldn't remember the last time Logan and I shared a can of corn. It had to be months ago. I pushed the thoughts out of my mind.

I decide it was best if I tried to hunt while I was still in the woods. I didn't know how many forests I would find on my journey, so I decided to save the cans for later. I set my backpack by a tree and covered it with leaves. I put my arrow sheath on my back and held my bow in my hands.

I stood behind a tree, a bush in front of me. I stayed quiet, listening to my surroundings. It was eerily quiet, a quiet I was never able to get used to. After two hours of waiting without a trace of movement or sound, I left the bush and returned to where I had left my backpack. Not a squirrel, bird, or even a mouse moved around me. Something was wrong.

When I found the tree where I left my backpack, I stopped in my tracks. It was gone. Where was my backpack? I thought. I heard a stick snap behind me. I turned around, bow at the ready, and froze.

Standing in front of me was a boy. He was about five-ten with shaggy brown hair and brown eyes. He had my backpack on his back and was dressed simply. His t-shirt was torn around the bottom, and his shorts had dirt smudges. His blue Nike's were hardly blue anymore and you could tell he'd been out in the woods for a while. In his left hand was a handgun and in his right, a rabbit. The thing I noticed the most about him though was the long scar traveling from his ankle all the way up his leg until it disappeared under his shorts.

I didn't lower my bow and I stared at him suspiciously. He never raised his gun or even looked surprised to see me. He was rather calm. Too calm. "Who are you?" I asked. He stepped towards me. I raised my bow higher. "Don't move. Who are you?" I repeated.

"I'm Carter. Carter Jones," he said.

"Give me my backpack," I spat at him. He looked over his shoulder and smiled.

"Is this yours?" he asked. He took it off his back and stepped closer to me.

"Don't move," I warned, still holding my bow up.

"You should really do a better job at disguising these things," he said. "An animal could see this from miles away. And it's pink. Not the best color when you are hiding in the woods – or anywhere for that matter."

"Be quiet and throw it over here."

He tossed my backpack and it landed at my feet. I picked it up and slung it over my back.

"Well," he said, "what's your name?"

Rather than answering I only glared at him.

"Okay," he said, "um, you're the girl who lives in the white house a couple hundred yards that way, right?" He pointed towards my house.

"How'd you know that?" I asked.

"Nope, I won't answer any more of your questions until you answer some of mine. You live there with your brother, don't you? Why isn't he here with you?"

"Ana."

"Ana..." He trailed off, questioning me.

"Talley."

"Don't speak much, huh?"

"How'd you know where I lived?" I asked once again.

"I've seen you and you're brother hunting around in these woods before."

"How long have you been in my woods?" I asked, angry with myself that I'd never noticed him in the woods before.

"Oh, only about two weeks. I've been traveling all over for the last couple of months. I'm from Wanatah. Are you going to put that bow down anytime soon?" He laughed. It was a low chuckling that was so unexpected it made me slowly lower my bow.

"Why are you out here, Carter?" I asked. "Where are your parents?"

He sighed and looked me in the eye. "My dad disappeared. I've been on my own for the last six months. How about you? Where are your parents?"

"Gone. They abandoned us—me." My throat tightened and I had to stop talking to keep myself from tearing up. I refused to let Carter see me upset. I wouldn't show him a weak point.

Carter sat down and leaned against a tree. He pulled out a backpack of his own he had hidden in the bushes. It was wrapped around with vines and leaves and twigs. You couldn't see what the original color of it was. He pulled off all of the sticks and threw them in a pile on the ground. He added sticks and pulled out a Bic lighter to ignite the leaves and sticks. Soon he had a fire going. He pulled a knife out of his bag and used it to skin the rabbit.

I finally decided to sit down and leaned up against a tree across from him. He skewed the rabbit with a stick and set it over the fire. As I watched him cook it, my stomach started to grumble again. I looked around for a mint leaf but couldn't find one. The cooked rabbit sent a smell wafting into the air. My stomach started to ache with emptiness.

He took the rabbit off the fire and cut it with his knife. I watched him as he ate the first piece of rabbit and I couldn't stand it anymore. I started to stand up, but he spoke first.

"Wait, sit down. I have plenty." He cut off a few pieces of meat and walked them over to me. "I was going to share with you, but I had to make sure it was all the way finished."

I took the food from him and ate the first piece. Flavor exploded in my mouth. I swallowed it and forced myself not to just shovel the rest of the rabbit in my mouth. I slowly chewed each piece until it was gone. When I was done I looked up to find Carter watching me.

"What?" I asked.

"Well, I was just wondering. You never answered my question."

"What?"

"Where is your brother?"

I looked away. "He's the reason I'm out here. He disappeared. But not like my parents. He would never abandon me. His room was torn apart, and there was a trail leading into our woods. I don't know what happened, but I know something's happened to him."

He looked at me suspiciously. "You say there was a trail?" I nodded my head.

"Can you show me?"

CHAPTER 9

CARTER

WE RAN BACK to the house where I threw my backpack on the ground and sprinted to where the trail started. Ana was right. Logan's room is messy – but it could have just been messy because he was too lazy to clean it. The only odd thing was that his sheets were on the ground. I told Ana this and an expression of hurt crosses her face.

"My brother wasn't a slob." she defended him. "I'm telling you the truth, something happened to him. You have to believe me!"

I held my hands up in front of me, "I'm not accusing him of anything I was just asking!" I turned before she could say anything else and I followed the trail down the hallway. There were shelves lining the wall and there were a few bins out of place; one was knocked over, but not any severe damage that would lead to what I had in mind.

When we reached the door, I noticed the screen was missing. It was frayed along the edges of the door showing it had been torn out. "Have you located the screen?" I asked Ana. She shook her head yes and pointed to the screen lying in the flower bed next to the door.

The tracks begin there in the frozen mulch. Like Ana told me on the way to the house, it looked like something was being dragged. I squatted down on the ground to get a better look at the tracks. I already knew which way the thing was heading, but I wanted to see if I could find any specific details about the trail, and I wanted to make Ana think I really knew what I was doing so I continued concentrating.

She looked different up-close than she did viewed from afar. Her baby-like features were more defined, hinting that she was a lot stronger than she appeared to be. Her light brown hair which was probably even lighter, maybe a tint of blonde, in the summer time hung loosely just past her shoulders. Her tiny figure that was about five foot two made her seem even more delicate. I knew she wasn't though if she and her brother had survived this long on their own.

I know she was determined too. I saw her chopping wood one day while I was resting while Logan hunted. It looked difficult for her to repeatedly swing the ax but she kept swinging until three logs were broken. Then when she was walking she started to drop all the wood and I was about to stand up and help her when Logan suddenly appeared and picked up the wood.

I snapped out of my day dreaming when Ana asked, "Do you notice anything?"

"Well, I need to follow the rest of the trail to where it stops in the woods before I can be sure." We continued walking down the trail and she inspected it right behind me. Half-way to the woods there was an indentation bigger than my foot. I was curious then and also a tiny bit worried. When the trail finished at the end of the woods I decided I knew what had happened.

"Ana, can I ask you a question?"

"Sure," she said in a monotonously.

"Where did your parents work?" She became almost angry.

"I don't know why this has anything to do with Logan-"

"It has everything to do with Logan." I argued.

"They were scientists."

I paused from what I heard. *Oh no.* My accusation was right.

"I found it," I whispered.

"Found what?"

"What happened to your brother. Did you go all the way to the woods when following the trail?"

"Yes, but I wasn't paying a whole lot of attention to it, just walking beside it."

"Then you wouldn't have seen it if you hadn't been studying the ground closely."

"Seen what?" Ana exclaimed.

"The print," I whispered.

"What?"

"Ana, the beast took your brother."

CHAPTER 10

LOGAN

THE PAIN IN my leg was unbearable. I gritted my teeth and sat up. I coughed as I breathed in smoke.

Where am I?

Looking around I tried to find an answer, but the haze and smoke were too thick. I tried to shout for Ana, but my throat burned and nothing but a hoarse whisper escaped. My mouth was dry, lips cracked. I needed water. I tried to stand, but I crumpled to the ground the moment I stepped onto my left leg. My jeans were ripped and blood soaked around the bottoms. Tentatively rolling up what was left of my pant leg I found rows of bite marks traveling up my calf. Something bit me – hard.

What happened to me?

The last thing I remembered was going to sleep last night. Or was it two nights ago? Was it a week ago? I didn't have any idea what day it was. *Where was Ana?* I hoped she was at home. *How far away was home?*

My stomach rumbled and I tried to peer through the smoke to focus on something, anything. I needed to eat, and I needed water. I ripped off the shredded parts of my jeans and tied them around my leg. I tried to stand up again, but I heard a deep growl which startled me back to the ground.

Red eyes stared at me through the smoke. The growling continued, sending shivers up my spine, and I tried to scoot back, away from those eyes, but everytime I moved, it growled. All of a sudden the eyes disappeared. I blinked to see if I could see them again through the smoke, but I couldn't see anything.

Cautiously I scooted on my butt an inch backwards, and when I dudn't hear a growl I scooted again – still nothing. I continued moving a few feet back until I hit something. Warm air was on my neck and I turned my head to find myself staring straight into those evil, red eyes. A black snout was inches from my face. Its head was enormous. Twice the size of my head.

Fear knocked the wind out of me like a tornado so I couldn't breathe. Scooting back on my butt, it growled and grabbed ahold of my bad leg. I let out a scream, the pain was excruciating. It dragged me backwards until I was once again sitting in front of it. I looked back at my leg to see that the wound had reopened. Blood rushed out. The animal paused, staring off into space and then snapped back to reality. It bounded away and I was able to get a good look at it. It must have been at least seven feet tall with strong muscles rippling underneath its coat.

It was gone for a few minutes, but then it returned, jumping over my head and turning to face me. It leaned in close my face, and did something I will remember forever.

"Stay put," it said.

CHAPTER 11

ANA

By NOW THE sun was gone from the sky and the moon was peeking out from behind the trees. Carter and I were back at my house. Not where I wanted to be, but where I had to be. We made a fire in the fireplace and were sitting on our couch. I knew I need to sleep, but my mind was far too awake to even think about getting any. After Carter blurted out about this beast thing, his eyes had a terrified look in them. They reminded me how my dad's eyes looked the last day I saw him. Then Carter grabbed my hand and he ran for the house.

"What do you mean the beast took him?" I asked angrily. "What is the beast?"

"Shh!" Carter hissed. "Don't be so loud! We have to figure this out rationally. That trail might be the biggest thing we have."

"The biggest thing we have for what?" I whispered.

"Look, I know you are confused right now," Carter says, "but you have to listen to me without intcrupting me. If I ask you a question, I need you to answer with complete honesty and with everything you know. Okay?"

"Okay, but-"

"No. Just listen."

I nodded my head and leaned back on the couch, annoyed but decided that if I wanted any answers I had better do what he said.

"My dad was a scientist. He worked for a group called GSF – Global Scientists Foundation. They worked with thousands of other scientists across the globe to help save our Earth. They were very secretive about everything they did though. Everyday my dad would come home from work, and I would ask him what he did that day, but he couldn't tell me. All he ever said was, "It's confidential."

"I tried not to let it get to me, I tried to ignore it, but I was too curious. Right before World War III, my dad started coming home later and later. He was always distracted – frantic sometimes – and it made me nervous.

"Finally one day I walked into his office at home to see what he was doing. He was working at his computer typing away, fast and furious. He didn't even notice me enter. I had to say his name three times before his looked up from his computer. He asked me what I needed and after a deep breath and a mini pep talk before hand, I flat out asked him. I needed to know what was going on. What was he doing at work that was so important that he would come home from work just to ignore me and continue working, shut away in his office for hours? We sat in silence for a long time. Then he went through the house and locked all the doors. He closed all the curtains and when he came back into his office, he locked that door behind him.

"He made me swear I wouldn't repeat any of the things he was about to tell me. He spoke quickly in a rushed whisper. He told me to stay away from GSF, that no matter what, I was never to take a job there or in any way get involved with them.

"He then told me that World War III was coming. He couldn't tell me how GSF knew; only that he knew. He said he and two other scietists, Dan and Sue Talley, were partnered up to work on an experiment. It was to help the USA win World War III. They were given DNA samples and they preformed hundreds of expirements. All leading up to their greatest weapon – the beast – or their scientific label: BS-221.

"What is the beast? You are probably asking. It is what it is: a beast. It's the combination of a wolf, rottweiler, and many others I can't remember, all genetically mutated to grow to exuberant amounts, far exceeding any other creature. Not only was it big, but it was fast, strong, with heightened senses and quick reflexes. It was lethal. They put a chip in its brain so the scientists could train it without having to go near it. Even they were afraid of it.

"They were in the middle of creating a second beast when World War III finally hit. The science lab was in Chicago – so was one of the bombs. The scientists had moved the completed beast away before the bomb hit, but they couldn't move all of their equipment or BS-222. BS-222 was destroyed along with all of their experiments, data and knowledge of BS-221."

Carter paused. I hadn't moved an inch the whole time he had been talking and I realized I was holding my breath. I let it out and tried to focus. I must have a horrified look on my face because when I finally glanced up at Carter, he showed a mix of concern and sympathy.

My parents did this.

"I just want to make sure," Carter said, "Your parents are Dan and Sue Talley, right?"

I nodded my head because I knew that even if I tried no words would come out of my mouth.

"Well, I want to apologize first off," he continued. I stared at him, now my face in an expression of wonder. What would he need to apologize for?

"I know why your parents were taken. My dad too. They had been sworn to secrecy and my father broke that promise. Not an hour after he told me, the house was lit up with a light so blinding you couldn't see a thing. I became dazed and confused and eventually I fell asleep or passed out, I'm not sure which.

"I don't remember much of the white lights because I was locked in my room, but when I woke up my dad was gone. It wasn't hard to put two and two together. I waited a month for him to come back, but he never did. I decided it wasn't good for me to be couped up waiting all the time, so I left.

"Why I'm apologizing is this: when you told me your parents disappeared I thought it was weird for them to just leave. Then you told me your name, that your brother was gone, and now you confirmed that your parents were scientists. I just connected the dots. And I think that because my dad told the secret, the head of GSF was afraid your parents would tell you about the beast, so he took them too. Now, were you locked in a room the night your parents left?"

"No," I whispered.

"Oh, well how about Logan?"

"No."

"I think my dad tried to hide me from the scientists. Or maybe they didn't care, but since your parents never told you about the beast GSF probably didn't feel it was necessary to take you."

"That's..." I started but trailed off.

"Not good." Carter finished for me. "And I'm sorry. I'm sorry for everything you've had to go through."

"Well, Carter, okay. But, where did the beast take Logan, and why?"

Carter thought about this. After a few minutes and a deep breath he answered. "Well after the bombing, they had relocated their studies and they moved to Gary, Indiana. I would assume that's where he is."

"But Gary is a wasteland!"

"Exactly, that's why it's perfect to train the beast there. There are cement walls all around it to keep the thing trapped inside and it's just and old waste yard."

"If there is a cement wall, how did the beast get out?"

"That part I don't know yet, Ana. Anyways, I told you the scientists chipped it right?" I nodded. "Well, they can talk to the beast through it," he paused.

"I think the scientists sent the beast to Logan."

Chapter 12

Sue

"WHERE IS THE water!" I screamed at Dan and Jesse. "Get him some water!" I leaned over my desk and watched the monitor. *My poor baby.* I glanced up at Dan and Jesse who were just standing around. I spun around to face them. "Don't just stand there! Why isn't it back with water? Where's all the food? Where are the bandages? Anything! Go!" I yelled, furious at how clueless they were.

Jesse walked over and sat by the microphone. He told it to get Logan to the stream, but nothing more.

"Well?" I asked.

"We're working on it," said Jesse, "It was a bigger explosion then we had planned for."

"Obviously!" I was so frustrated I could slap them. "Who else is helping us fix this?"

Dan and Jesse glance at each other, then back at me. "Only one," Jesse said.

"Who!"

"My son."

CHAPTER 13

ANA

I STOOD UP, FURIOUS. "My parents wouldn't do that! Logan is their *son*! You don't even know my parents! How could you make accusations like that?" I spat at Carter.

"I'm sorry, Ana, and you are probably right. I shouldn't have said anything. I'm just trying to figure this out. I'm in the same situation that you are in, in case you forgot."

"No you're not! Your brother wasn't supposedly taken by some beast!"

"SHH! Don't speak so loud about that!"

"Why shouldn't I?" I can't keep my voice down I'm too furious.

"Look, Ana, I'm sorry for anything I ever said to offend you. I didn't mean to hurt you in any way. I think we are both tired and we need some sleep."

"I'll sleep on the couch, you can have the floor," I huffed and grabbed a blanket. There was no need to pretend I cared about being a courteous host. I pushed everything Carter said out of my mind and eventually I was asleep.

"Ana!" Carter yelled. He was shaking me awake. My eyes snapped open and I sat up.

"Ana, we have to go!"

My eyes flew open to white. I was drowning in it. There was a tugging on my hand and then I noticed Carter pulling me up out of my bed and shoving my backpack in my hands. His backpack was already on his back and he ran to the door, dragging me with him.

"What the heck is going on?" I yanked my hand out of his and stopped.

"There's no time for explanations! Come on!"

"No! Where are we going?" I screamed at him.

"Shh! There is no time for stubbornness if you want to make it out of here alive." He turned around and grabs my shoulders, looking intently into my eyes. "How many ways out of here are there?" He whispered hastily.

"Umm, the door?" I respond sarcastically.

"No! I mean something not obvious!" He looks around. Then his face lit up. "Basement. Do you have basement?"

"Yeah, but –"

He yanked my arm so fast I almost fell. "Where is it?" He yelled frantically opening every door we passed.

"It's at the end of the hall!" I yelled. We raced to the end of the hall and sprinted down the basement stairs.

"Is there a door? A window?"

"There is a window over the washer and dryer in the back room!"

I led him through the main room to the laundry room in the back. The washer and dryer had been broken for months, so I hadn't even been back there in a long time. Carter stepped ahead of me and climbed on top of the washer. The window was half the size of a regular window and painted shut. Instead of wasting time by trying to chip off the paint he broke the window with a hammer he pulled out of his backpack. He punched out the screen and stuck his head out the small opening.

A few seconds later he pulled his head back inside and whispers that it's safe and we can go out this way. "I'll go first," he says, "to make sure everything really is safe." He climbed out then kneeled on the ground and waved his hand through and whispers, "Come on!"

I climbed onto the washing machine and grabbed his hand. He helped me through the window and we frantically looked around. In a way I didn't know was possible, the white light grew even brighter. I squinted and tried to gain my bearings. We were standing in a small alcove surrounded on two sides. One side was my brother's room, the other was our porch. I squinted at Carter to see which way he wanted to go. He was looking around, searching. There were two options. One: we run into town. Two: we run into the forest. I knew Carter was thinking the same thing because he whispered, "Woods!" I nodded my head and we crept out from our hiding spot.

We looked both ways when we were crossing the yard just like when you cross a street, only this time it was for a reason and not just out of habit, and then we were sprinting for the woods. All of a sudden the white light disappeared. Carter stopped dead in his tracks and I smashed into his back. "What!" I yelled. I took a step back, holding my head. I peeked around him and then I saw what Carter saw.

A man was stepping out from behind the first tree into our woods.

Then it started to rain.

CHAPTER 14

LOGAN

I OPENED MY EYES. The smoke was thinning, my head was pounding, and my leg was throbbing. It was raw, bleeding, and arduous. I must have passed out from blood loss. I pressed my hand to my head and when I pulled it away it was bloody. I must have hit my head when I fell back against the hard concrete.

I looked around and noticed a bucket. It was hardly blue anymore from all the dirt and dust. I attempted to pull it closer to me but pain shot from my arm to my skull. Slowly, taking deep breaths to try and even out my breathing and end the pain, I dragged the bucket to my side. Inside was water. I looked up to the sky and let out a sigh of relief. Dipping my hands in the water I scooped some out to pour over my head, on my arms, and into my mouth. The dry, dustiness left and instead I was filled with relief. I felt as though I could not drink enough water, but I knew it is vital to save some for my wound.

Carefully I poured some onto my leg. I drizzled the water down the length of the wound and while it stung at first, I gritted my teeth and kept going. I knew that the most important thing was to keep infection from spreading. If I wanted a nice, clean healing process I had to rinse it out. After covering my entire leg I ripped my shirt around the bottom and dunk it in the water. Then I wrapped it around my calf and breathed.

When I looked up I noticed the two red eyes staring at me through the haze.

CHAPTER 15

CARTER

THE MAN STOOD next to the trees and stared at us. All of a sudden I gasped.

"What?" Ana asked.

The man looked similar to my dad. "Dad?" I whispered. I started walking to the woods. The man had the same facial shapes except for the new beard he had grown. I started speed walking, then full out sprinting. "Dad!"

Ana quickly followed behind me but stayed back as we reached the woods. The man opened his arms wide and I ran into his embrace. Ana walked up as we were finishing our hugs and she stood awkwardly beside us, looking around to make sure no one else was here, in one sense out of protection and in another it seemed to be to keep her own hopes from rising.

"Dad," I said, "what are you doing here? How did you escape? What's going on?"

"Shh!" Carter's father warned us.

"What?" Ana asked.

"Sorry!" I whispered. "Dad this is Ana. Ana, meet my dad, Jesse."

"Hi, Ana," He said. She nodded her head to him but kept quiet.

"Look," Jesse said, "we don't have a lot of time. You two have to go. You have to leave."

"We were sorta in the middle of doing just that," Carter told him.

"Good! Where are you going?" Jesse asked us.

Ana decided to step in then. "We are trying to find my brother Logan. And maybe my parents."

"Oh no. No, no, no." Jesse whispered. "Ana. You're Ana Talley. You can't go after your parents. I wish I could tell you where they were, but a lot of bad things could happen if I did that. And your brother. You can't go after him either."

"What! Why not?"

"Again, I'm sorry. You just can't. I wish I could tell you why, but I would just be putting your brother in danger."

"So he's okay now? Do you know where he is?"

"I can't answer any of your questions. You are not asking the right questions. Listen to me when I tell you. Ignorance is bliss," my dad said.

"Well," I joined in the conversation again, "What do you think we should do if we can't go after Ana's brother?"

"We are going to find Logan!" Ana shouted. Too loud.

"Shh!" Dad quieted Ana. But it was too late. All of a sudden a dim light shined in the distance. We all stared at it. Watching it grow closer. "Oh, dang," he said. Only he doesn't use dang. "Okay, listen. No matter what, don't go after Logan. It is of the upmost importance that you stay away from him. I will do everything I can to help him, but you two have to get out of here. Now."

"Where are we supposed to go?" Carter asked.

"South. Get south. Go to Lafayette or Indianapolis. Find a shelter. Just leave! I'm going to stall the captain as long as I can," he paused and turned to Carter. "I love you, son." He hugged me and turned to leave.

"No!" I whispered hastily. "Come with us! I can't lose you again, Dad."

"Carter, I'm sorry. I have to go." He walked over to me and whispered in my ear, then dashed out towards the light.

I grabbed Ana's hand and pulled her along. We dashed through the forest to get away. We headed out into the wild.

"We have to stop!" Ana spoke slowly because she was winded. She put her hands on her head to catch her breath.

"We have only been running for a few miles," I told her.

"Well, unlike you I'm not some kind of super hero who can just take off and run a marathon."

I chuckled. "A marathon is twenty-six miles, Ana. We've only been running for about four." Finally her breathing returned normal and she plopped down on the ground.

"Four miles! That's my limit. That's more than I've ran in the two years combined! Plus, it's night time! I'm surprised I haven't tripped over a root and fallen flat on my face!"

"Well, the sun is coming up, so it will be easier to see as we run. We can't stop now." A small amount of daylight is growing brighter as we talk.

"I don't care. We need to eat," Ana argued with me. "We will just make a small fire here and heat up some tomato soup. I have one can left," she tempts me in a sing-song voice.

"I don't think so. Let's get farther south we are still in Valparaiso." I took her hand and pulled her up so she stood in front of me.

"Yeah, about that! We ran in the wrong direction! We have to double back so we can get to my brother!"

"No," I stopped her, "we have to go south like my dad said."

"What! You can't be serious!" She blurted out.

"Of course I'm serious." What did she think?

"We have to go get Logan!" She protested. "We aren't going to change our plans because some guy hiding in my back yard said we should!"

"That man is my father!" I couldn't help it, I was yelling now.

"And Logan is my brother!"

"I know and I think we have to head south! My dad said it's the best way to help him! I want to get him back just like you, and I think in order for him to stay safe we need to head south and get help!"

She paused and took a couple of deep breaths. I used the time to calm down too. Our yelling could've attracted the light.

"Let's just calm down," she started. "Let's camp out here for the night, then in the morning we can head… south."

44

CHAPTER 16

ANA

I CAN'T BELIEVE *I told Carter we would head south.* I couldn't fall asleep. Carter had no problem, he just rolled out his sleeping bag, stared at the stars for a minute, and then before I was even all the way in my sleeping bag, he was out. The sun was shining bright in the sky, and even though I only had a few hours of sleep the night before, I knew I wasn't going to get any now. I grabbed my bow and set off into the woods a little bit farther.

I found a comfy spot to hunt up in a sturdy ash tree. I wasn't up in that tree an hour before I heard crunches in the leaves. I loaded my bow and drew it back, aiming and waiting to see what would come out of the bushes in front of me. I almost let out a gasp in surprise. A raccoon stepped out. A raccoon! I quickly aim and release the arrow, sending it straight through its heart. I hopped out of the tree and retrieved it. It was not very fat, but it sure was the biggest animal I'd hunted in the last two months.

I carried my kill back to our "campsite" and found Carter still asleep. A nasty trick came to mind and I wiped the raccoon's tail across Carters face. When he started to stir, I set the animal on his chest so it was looking him directly in the eyes. I jumped behind the tree so he wouldn't see me. He didn't fully awaken, so I grabbed a stick on the ground next to me and poked his check hard. His eyes popped open and the first thing he saw was the raccoon.

"Ahhhh!" He screamed like a girl. He threw it off him and pulled out his hand gun.

"Stop!" I jumped out from behind the tree. He swung around, gun still in hand, and just about died.

"I can't believe you did that!" Carter yelled at me. I was too busy cracking up to respond. He put the gun away in his little sheath and became silent. His brows scrunched together and he scowled. "Where did you find that thing anyways?"

"A hundred yards that way." I pointed to where I was hunting while I picked up sticks to start a fire. "Could you start skinning that? I don't know about you, but I'm starving!"

Still scowling, Carter silently readied the raccoon and soon it was cooking over the warm fire. It's not the best meat I've had, but I was too hungry to care. Carter and I ate all of the raccoon and for the first time in months, I was full.

It felt wonderful to be able to say I was full. Although, my stomach surely wasn't as happy as I thought it would be. I might have eaten too much, and by Carter's expression I thought he felt the same way. It was better than feeling hungry I decided and I rolled up my sleeping bag.

Carter and I set off through the woods and soon we reached a road. Across it stood a rusty, dented sign that read Sixty-Five. I turned to Carter. "I'm pretty sure this road will take us all the way to Indianapolis."

"Are you ready?" he asked me.

"Ready for what? We're not even doing anything important. We are just walking." I scowled at him.

"You said we would go south. So, south it is."

"Fine, let's go."

We walked down the road the entire day. I was tired and we had traveled around fifteen miles in a few hours. We were passing the only other forest I had seen since we left and I was glad that raccoon stumbled in when it did.

All of a sudden something crashed through the forest – heading in our direction.

CHAPTER 17

CARTER

I TURNED AROUND AND saw a lady jump onto the road. She was wearing torn jean capris with a plain white t-shirt. Her hair was in a curly mess, part of it up in a ponytail with lots of stands falling out. She wasn't wearing any shoes and her feet were almost completely black from dirt, but also red which must have been dried blood from her feet getting torn up.

In her right hand was a knife which she raised as she stumbled towards us. Ana shrunk back with a look of horror on her face, but surprisingly, I stayed calm. When I was traveling before I reached Ana's house, I had an encountered with a boy probably a year younger than me who was going crazy trying to get food. That's probably what this lady wanted too.

Instead of fleeing, I took a stance of defense with one arm in front of me, the other reaching towards my gun, and stood on the balls of my feet so I could move quickly if I needed to. "It's okay," I said to the woman. "We are just passing through."

I called to the woman, louder, but I still wasn't getting any reaction from her. Instead she started slinking forward, head down, eyes up, stringy hair blowing across her nose. Her armed hand in front of her, the other out to the side she made her way towards us, low to the ground like a lion stalking its prey. The look of thirst and desire in her eyes, complete evil, revealed to me a determination unlike any I had seen before.

I pulled out my hand gun and pointed it at her. Still she did not stop. "If you go back home, everything will be fine." I tried. Ana held onto my backpack, I could feel her trying to tug me gently backwards so we could run. Unexpectedly the woman started full on sprinting at me, her cleaver reflecting the sunlight. She was only a few yards away and Ana screamed and took off down the road. I didn't want to, but I pulled the trigger. I hit her in the chest and she fell on her face while she was running. She dropped the knife and it slid across the ground, stopping at my feet. The lady didn't move or make any sounds, even when I walked over and cautiously poked her with my foot.

The blood was flowing out of her, pooling on the ground, and try as I might I could not stomach it. I turned away from her and hurled, the entirety of my stomach's contents were splashed out on the pavement. Finally I managed to spit everything out and stand back up, my knees wobbling. I looked and could see Ana waiting patiently down the street, sitting with her knees curled in and a void expression on her face.

I walked back towards her, picking up the knife on the way. Ana and I continued walking in silence. After another mile or so of walking, Ana broke the silence. "Why didn't you run away?" she asked me.

I shrugged my shoulders. "I've encountered it before."

"Is that how you got your scar?" She asked. I wasn't ready for that question and she must have noticed from my shocked expression. "I'm sorry," she said. "Sometimes I speak without thinking. You don't have to answer that."

I nodded my head thanks. "I'll tell you when I feel the time is right. You need to know, just not now."

I knew Ana understood and we kept on in silence. It wasn't a bad silence, it was comfortable. We walked like that for the next hour until the sun went down. We had passed up the woods, so we decided to sleep on the side of the road. Since there weren't any cars, we both agreed that we didn't think it would be a problem.

My sleeping bag did little to add any comfort to my back. The pavement was hard and the gravel bit into my neck. No matter how many pieces of gravel I wiped away, I always found more that slipped into my sleeping bag and into my hair. After an hour of tossing and turning with no sleep to be found I gave up, exasperated. I looked over at Ana and saw that she wasn't sleeping either, although she was much quieter than I had been.

"What's the point of just laying here, when we could be traveling?" I asked.

She turned over and faced me. "There isn't one. Do you want to keep going?"

"Why not?" We rolled up our bags and set off again in the dark. I pulled out my flashlight and looked at Ana. "Do you have a flashlight?"

"Yeah, good idea!" She reached into her bag and rummaged around until she pulled out a simple black flashlight. She turned it on and a stronger beam of light shot out than I thought possible for such a small flashlight. "It feels weird to be walking down an empty street at night and not hear any sounds except for our footsteps," she thought aloud. It was just a statement, but I felt like I should respond anyways.

"It does. World War III was... what? Ten months ago? One year ago did you ever think you would be walking down the highway at night in the middle of an empty country?"

"Well that's a hard question!" Ana laughed sarcastically, "Last year I thought that I would be driving now, and that I would have this huge sweet sixteen with all my friends and a DJ with bright lights and maybe get a refurbished yellow Volkswagen beetle from that old model which came out in 2070 for my present. I'd be allowed to go out on dates and I wanted to go to prom and get my first kiss."

"You haven't been kissed yet?" I asked shocked.

"It doesn't matter!" She said defensively. Instead she changed the subject. "What about you? What were you planning?"

"Well, I've already had my sixteenth birthday. I was looking forward to finishing junior year and taking blow off classes as a senior. I finally made the varsity soccer team and I wanted to go to state. I had a girlfriend, but I don't know where she is now. Everyone just sort of vanished, you know? But I had a car, it was a crappy car —"

"What car?" Ana asked me.

I whispered very quietly, "A Chevy."

"No!" she burst out laughing.

"That car company got shut down like forty-five years ago for all of their fraud models and parts! Where did you even find one?"

"My grandpa bought it for me. I have no clue where he got it. It was probably in his back yard for thirty years." I started laughing remembering the sight of it. "My girlfriend didn't even want to ride in it. It was this rusty color and the doors creaked every time you opened it and it only had forty mpg's! It was pretty bad."

Ana burst out laughing at me.

"Stop laughing! You haven't even been kissed yet!"

Ana sobered up instantly. "Truce," she asked and stuck out her hand.

"Truce," I shook her hand.

"Hey, look!" Ana suddenly called.

CHAPTER 18

LOGAN

SOMETIME LATER A rumbling woke me up. I sat up and realized it was my stomach. Hunger pains tore through me. I gripped my sides and looked around me. I noticed that next to the water bucket was a few pieces of hard bread. I dragged myself over to them and stuffed one of the pieces into my mouth. I had to force myself not to shovel them down all at once. My stomach only groaned more so I ate two more pieces, left the three last pieces and decided I would eat those tomorrow or even the day after if I could make them last. There was still water in the bucket so I unwrapped my shirts and dunked them so they would soak.

My leg was growing in size from swelling and around the bites it was turning red. The pain wasn't getting better, but I was dealing with it. My head was pounding though. I gingerly touched the back of my head and intense pain shot through me all the way down my spine. I didn't know what to do for that injury, so I decided to leave it and see what happened. I tried to stand up, but the pain in my head and my leg was too much. I quickly sat back down on the ground and stared at my surroundings. I had no idea where the beast thing went. All I knew was that I need to get out. Soon.

CHAPTER 19

ANA

I SHINED MY FLASHLIGHT onto the side of the road and almost jumped for joy. Instead I grabbed Carter's arm and started running down the road. There on the side of the road was a model pack. When we reached it I quickly opened up the large model. A model pack was like buying a traveling house that included a car but didn't have a roof, and if the car was a hover board.

They came with a hover board which was like a snowboard but it flew through the air, food that could not spoil, fire starter kits, coats, boots, flashlights, medical kits, and VCR's: Video Communication Rocks. VCR's look like flat rocks but you can talk to people through video chat on them. I had always wanted one.

When we opened up the model pack, it was safe to say I was disappointed. All that was left were a couple of Band-Aids and some bread crumbs. I'd always wanted to ride a hover board. Logan had been saving his money for one, but he hadn't even come close by the time WWIII hit. I threw the Band-Aids in my backpack and stood up. I was about to trudge away and let myself be disappointed when Carter stopped me.

"Have you ever used a model pack?" He asked me.

"No, I couldn't afford one of those things."

"Well, my friend used to have one and if I remember correctly..." he felt around the inside with his hand until, "Yes! I found it!"

I ran over to him and in his hand he was holding two VCR's. "Where were those?"

"In the secret compartment! Obviously whoever this belonged to didn't know about it either. Here, turn yours on and see if it works."

I quickly hit the power button in the right hand corner and a light lit up my face in the darkness. I programmed it to channel three and once it was loaded, I saw Carter's face.

"Hey!" He said.

"Can you believe our luck?" I asked him through the VCR.

"Of course not," he laughed. "Go down the road a couple yards to make sure these really work and I'm not just hearing your voice since you are right in front of me."

I jogged down the road and when I could just barely see Carter, I looked at the VCR. "Can you hear me?" I asked him.

"Yes!" Carter exclaimed.

"These can help us so much."

"I know, now we can split up to hunt and we don't have to worry about anything."

"I know, I know!" I almost jumped up and down, but since Carter could see me through the VCR I decided not to.

"Come back over here and we will check out the rest of this model pack."

I turned off my VCR and I sauntered back to Carter. I'm so happy for the first time since Logan played his guitar for me a week ago. When I reached Carter he was inspecting the bag carefully, but he didn't find anything else hidden anywhere.

He said, "I can't believe we were able to find VCR's. What kind of idiot would buy a model pack and not know to open the pouch where the VCR's are?"

"I didn't know where they were."

Carter quickly tried cover up his words, "Yeah, but you didn't buy the model pack, you just found one. I don't think anyone would expect you to know everything that comes in a model pack."

"Yeah, yeah, whatever," I said. Even though Carter's words had stung, just being able to have some kind of technology in my hands made me so happy, I decided not to let his words get to me.

Carter looked at me to make sure I was okay. Since I was smiling, he knew my feelings weren't hurt too badly. "Look, the sun is coming up. We can turn off our flashlights before we leave." We stuffed our flashlights away and stood up. "Do you have your VCR?" Carter asked me. I nodded. "Alright then, let's get going."

All of a sudden we heard a gun cock.

CHAPTER 20

CARTER

ANA AND I instantly stopped walking.

Then a gruff voice said, "I wouldn't be leaving if I were you,"

Ana frantically whispered, "What do we do!"

"I would say we don't leave," I whispered back. I wanted to reach for my gun, but I didn't want the man to know that I was armed. He might have shot us right on the spot.

"Turn around!" He yelled.

We turned around slowly and on the side of the road behind the model pack was a man about five foot ten wearing jeans and a ratty t-shirt. His dirty blonde hair has grown to just above his shoulders and his five o'clock shadow had turned into a full-on beard.

He pointed his gun at us and waved it towards him, beckoning us to come closer. Ever so slowly, Ana and I crept forward towards the man.

"Hold out your hands!" he commands us.

Ana and I both know it wouldn't be a good idea to show him empty hands, so we both held out our arms to him and uncurled our fingers from around the VCR's. He snatched them and put them in his pocket.

Then he pointed his gun at Ana's temple. My hand surreptitiously slid towards my handgun.

"Alright, listen up," he instructed. He turned to me. "You are going to walk right in front of me. And you," he turned and put his face right into Ana's, "you are going to stay right by me. Got it?" I started walking and I watched him yank Ana from where she was standing causing her to let out a small yelp in surprise. He jerked her to a stop, so I stopped too. "I don't want a peep out of you little miss." And then turning his attention to me after noticing my pause he yelled, "And you! Keep walking!"

I tentatively took a step forward, listening for the sound of Ana moving behind me and when I finally heard two more sets of footsteps behind me I continued to walk forward at a more constant pace. After half an hour of walking, the man said to go right. I turned right and we passed under two trees and into a wood. The man pushed Ana to the ground and I instantly turned to face him. I was about to yell at him to stop hurting Ana, when he yelled, "Shut up, boy! Sit down right there!"

I crossed my legs and plopped to the ground. The man lit a fire next to me and pulled out a can of beans. The entire time his gun rested firmly in his hand. He ate in front of us, and I knew he was enjoying the sensation of knowing that we were hungry and he didn't have to share his food with us.

Hours passed by, an entire day wasted and all this man did was eat his beans and stare at us. I was beyond frustrated.

"Whats your name, boy?" He asked me when he finished eating. I didn't respond or even look at him. "I said, what's your name boy!" He hollered once more. Again, I simply ignored him. I heard him grunt and I heard his footsteps draw nearer. He leaned down to my level and instead of his gun, he produced a knife. He touched it to my cheek, and pushed it in. "I said, what's your name boy?" When I didn't respond he began adding pressure to my cheek until I felt it penetrate. He slit my cheek open and waited.

"Carter." I finally say.

"That's better. That wasn't too hard. When you listen to me and do what I say, we can all get along very nicely now, can't we." He said it as a statement rather than a question, inferring that we were going to "get along" whether we liked it or not because if we didn't get along, we wouldn't exist.

Blood dripped from my cheek and ran down my face. Some reached my lip and I could taste the saltiness of it. My cheek burned but I refused to let him know he hurt me. He stood up and returned to his bag. He pulled out a rope that he had cut in half and yanked my wrists. He bound them first and then my ankles second.

Over the man's shoulders I could see Ana watching me. She touched her cheek to see if I was okay where my cheek was cut. I nodded my head thanks. She leaned back against the tree and closed her eyes. Once the man was done securing the rope around my ankles he walked over to Ana. I hoped he didn't tie her ropes as tight as he tied mine. My wrists were already beginning to sting.

He paused in front of Ana and began talking to her, eventually choosing to take a seat. She was too far away and he was speaking to quietly for me to hear what they were discussing. I lied down on my back and looked up at the stars that were beginning to appear. There were faint clouds in the sky and I knew that the stars weren't going to shine very brightly that night.

My gaze focused back on Ana and the man when I heard footsteps once again. I saw him walking back to his fire and he unrolled a sleeping bag. Upon closer inspection I noticed it was my sleeping bag! He took my backpack and apparently felt free to use anything inside of it. Then the thought hit me. *The beans he ate were my beans!* This outraged me. I looked over to Ana to point it out when, to my surprise, I noticed she wasn't tied up.

CHAPTER 21

ANA

I THOUGHT ABOUT WHAT Michael York said. And first I wondered if that was even his real name. Though he did not tie me up I had no wish to run away. I looked over to see if Carter had fallen asleep and I caught his gaze. He glared at me. I gave him a puzzled look because I didn't understand what I did to cause him to become angry with me. Eventually he broke his gaze from mine and turned his head away and returned it uncomfortably back down on the ground.

I close my eyes and thought. He must have been angry because I was not tied up and he was, although it's not like I was in control of it. And it's not like I was mouthing off to York or disobeying him. If only he knew. If only he knew. I would rather be tied up than have the responsibility that now rested upon me.

I couldn't possibly fall asleep after the conversation Michael York and I had. After he slit open Carter's cheek and tied him up, he came over to talk to me. I was expecting to get tied up or brought closer to the fire near him and Carter. Instead, he sat down and got comfortable. He waited a minute, pondering what he was going to say. He didn't beat around the bush.

"I'm not going to tie you up," he said.

This took me by surprise. "Why?" I asked.

He chuckled, a horrible, cruel chuckle that was in no way leading to something funny. "See those ropes over there?" He pointed at Carter over his shoulder. "Well, let's just say they are a little invention of mine. I'd like to say I'm somewhat of an entrepreneur. See here," he pulled a little black sensor out of his pocket. The sensor had a strap and he grabbed my ankle. He quickly fastened it shut.

I took another look at it. I couldn't find the place where it hooked together. A quizzical expression came over me and I pondered how to get it off my ankle.

"Oh, that can't come off," he said, chuckling that cruel laugh.

"What!" I stood up, holding out my leg and attempting to examine it better.

"Oh, I wouldn't go too far. That sensor is also part of my invention. It is synched with that rope tied around Carter. If you get thirty feet away from him, this sensor will trace it and it will send a signal to that rope telling it so." He smirked.

"What happens then?" I asked quietly, afraid of what his answer will be.

"You can say bye-bye to lover boy. That signal will cause a little time box inside one section of the rope to catch fire. That flame travels down a teeny-tiny wire to the edge of the box and… BOOM."

"Boom?" I whispered hoarsely.

"Bye-bye lover boy."

I thought about what he told me. Anger and fear were mixing together, causing me to speak before thinking. "First of all, I don't know where you got the idea that he's Lover Boy. Second, we can still get away. We just have to stand right next to each other."

"Is that so?"

"That's what you just said." I cross my arms and glared at him. Inside I was kicking myself for speaking so bluntly.

He slapped his forehead. "Did I forget to mention the most important part? That sensor of yours, if it gets thirty-five feet away from me, sends a signal to this." He pulls a little hand-held black sensor from his pocket. "And I can hit this button right here, and – BOOM. Bye-bye to you and lover boy."

I swear my jaw dropped. He patted my knee and stood up, tilted an invisible hat like cowboys used to, and returned to his spot by the fire. *What are we going to do? York could be mentally insane for all we know, and now he has us connected to a bomb!*

I noticed Carter move and I tried to get his attention. He sat up and rubbed his ankles, clearly annoyed. They must have been hurting, tied up in that rope. When he finished he looked up at me. I motioned for him to come over by me, but all he did was scowl then lie back down and turn away from me.

I wanted to stand up and march over to him and tell him everything, but I knew that if I made that kind of scene York would be on us like hawks, and though he didn't tell me that I couldn't tell Carter, he probably didn't want me to. If I told Carter about the bombs, there would be major consequences to pay.

CHAPTER 22

LOGAN

MY BREAD WAS quickly gone. I knew it was not the right thing to do, but I couldn't help eating the rest of my bread the next day. I was hungrier than I'd ever been and the bread was sitting right next to me, tempting me, calling my name.

Frustrated that I couldn't control myself I decided to focus on cleaning my wound. I untied my shirt to clean up my leg and what I saw was horrifying. My leg was completely red and twice the size of the other leg. Obviously I needed more than water for this to heal.

There was nothing I could do about my leg though. All I had was a bucket that which quickly running out of water, and no food. *How was I going to get better so I could escape? And where did that beast go?*

I used my good leg to help scoot myself backwards. I moved a few feet and didn't hear any growls. That beast must have left. I tried to stand up so I could plan my escape, but my leg was throbbing and seemed to weigh a thousand pounds. Once I maneuvered myself back on the ground, I began to think. I scanned my surroundings and tried to accumulate a plan to escape.

I didn't get too far though because I heard a crash, a growl, and a thump.

And then next to me was a girl.

CHAPTER 23

CARTER

I WAS ROUSED AWAKE by a foot prodding my back. I groaned and rolled over. That man was standing above me, staring out at the forest beyond, and kicking me with his dark leather boots. I pulled myself up into a sitting position and stared at him. "What." It was an annoyed sound rather than a question.

"Get up," he said in his gruff voice.

I leaned myself forward until I fell on my hands and knees so I could jump up on my hands and feet and then finally crouch and push myself up. It was hard to move without the use of your arms and legs.

"We are leaving. Get your stuff and let's go," he ordered.

"How am I supposed to walk?"

"Jump up and down."

"You can't be serious!"

"Oh, I've never been more serious," he smiled cruelly.

I hopped over to my backpack. "How am I supposed to carry this if I can't get it on my back?"

"Will you stop complaining?" He spat at me.

"No."

"Usually I'm not this generous, but for today, I'll cut off the ropes around your feet. I don't want to be stuck listening to you complain all day." He bent down and inspected the rope. Once he found an easy spot to cut, he gingerly sliced through the rope. Once he finished cutting it, he looked inside and felt all the way around it.

I stopped paying attention to him though because my ankles were burning and I bent down to massage them. Part of the rope had been wrapped around my wound and that's where it stung the most. I was out of antibiotic cream and I didn't have anything else to put on it so I had to suck it up and deal with the pain.

I straightened back up and saw Ana approaching me. She had her backpack slung over one shoulder and she was free to move without any restraints. I was so angry about it I didn't even want to look at her. She stopped next to me anyways.

"We need to talk," she said.

I refused to acknowledge her in any way. The silent treatment might have been a little childish but it didn't keep me from resorting to it.

"Carter?" She pressed.

Nothing.

"I'm serious. This is important. Why won't you look at me?"

I'm too angry that's why. Then Ana got a mix of a hurt expression and an angry expression on her face and walked away. I saw one of her hands reach up to her face near her eye then quickly return back by her side. It was done quickly and discretely, obviously not wanting anyone to notice. *Is she crying?* All of a sudden I was filled with guilt. Ana and I were both stuck in the same situation only my hands were tied together. Even so, she must have been so scared. I didn't even know what that guy said to her. Maybe he threatened her in some way and I hadn't even taken the time to find out. We weren't looking for her brother and now we were kidnapped and I was ignoring her. She must have felt very alone. I made up my mind to talk to her sometime that day as long as that guy wasn't around.

He picked up my backpack and slung it on his shoulders. I sighed and walked towards him and Ana.

"Which way are we going?" I asked.

"East."

"No!" Ana yells, "We can't go east! We have to go south! Or even west!"

"I don't think so little miss."

"Yes I think so!" Ana argued back. She crossed her arms and I saw that look in her eyes: complete stubbornness with a mix of determination that the guy obviously saw as disobedience and defiance.

Oh no.

The man slapped her hard against the cheek. Ana's neck turned with it and instantly a red hand mark was left on her face. He then pulled out his knife and pointed it at Ana. "I don't think you heard me correctly. We are heading east."

Ana gulped and nodded her head, quickly backing off and keeping her eyes on the ground.

"That's better. Now, you boy! Out in front. And little miss, I want you behind him and I'll follow last. I don't think there will be any monkey business, now will there?" He gave Ana a sly smile and she looked away from him.

We set out and no one talked. The only time that man spoke was when that man busied himself barking orders at me because I was going the wrong way or walking too slow or too fast. I couldn't help it though, he didn't tell me where to walk, just that I had to.

By the time the day was over, I was starving. I hadn't eaten in over two days and that man still had my backpack. Ana must have felt the same way because she spoke up. "I'm starving, York! Is it possible we could stop and eat something?"

York? I thought.

York thought about this for a minute, let out a sigh, and then sat down my backpack. He unzipped it and pulled out a hunting gun, a handgun, and a pistol. I hadn't seen him pack all of his guns into the backpack. We could be in more danger than I imagined. Besides the gun he pulled out three more knives and some stray arrows. He handed the arrows to Ana who already had her bow out, and gave me a knife.

As he handed me the knife he said, "Now don't hurt yourself, boy." I scowled and he chuckled.

"I can't hunt with my hands tied up."

"I know. You can be our watch dog. Alright, now we are going to hunt in a triangle." He threw his backpack into a bush then grabbed Ana's and did the same thing. "Follow me."

We walked a few feet into the woods and York stopped. "Lover boy here." He pushed me into a bush and kept walking. Ten feet later he told Ana to climb up into a tree. He walked adjacent of her and rested behind a bush, leaning against a tree.

I felt useless and I could feel my anger and jealousy resurfacing as I watched Ana shoot a squirrel with a bow and York shoot a bird with his gun. In order to cope I took a nap.

Once the sun was fully out of site, Ana climbed down from the tree and York stomped over to me. "You weren't much help," he hissed.

"My hands are tied up! They've been tied up for two days!"

All York did was laugh.

We made a camp and York started a fire. Since I didn't hunt I was ordered to pluck the feathers out of York's bird and try to skin Ana's squirrel. It was problematic because of my hands.

"York?" I called to him.

He grunted in response.

"Can you please untie my hands while I eat? You're right here I'm not going to try to run away."

York contemplated my proposition, clearing weighing the advantages and disadvantages of untying me. He must have been confident in his abilities to keep me around because to my surprise York walked over and untied my wrists. But then he bent over and he tied my ankles again. "I'm not taking any chances with you, boy."

I could have been angry about having my legs tied up again, but I was too relieved to have free arms. The ropes had cut into my wrists and left marks, almost breaking the skin. I gently massaged each wrist for a few minutes but eventually gave up because they were too sore to really touch.

I stretched and did a few push-ups. My arms were becoming so weak! I hadn't exercised in a long time. After ten pushups I looked up and saw Ana watching me. I forgot about the pain because I wanted to impress her, so I did fifteen more. My arms were wobbling, but I ignored them. I acted as if it were easy. Then I let out a deep breath and sat back down to eat my bit of squirrel and bird, eventually laying down and looking up at the stars.

Since I took a nap when we were hunting today I couldn't fall asleep. I heard loud snores coming form York and I sat up. Ana was resting against a tree and watching me. I waved her over and after a glance towards York, reassuring herself that it was safe, she stood up and came towards me.

CHAPTER 24

ANA

CARTER MOTIONED FOR me to join him and against my better judgment, I did. I crossed my legs and sat down next to him. We sat in silence for a long time. I wanted to stay mad at him and ignore him, but my curiosity finally got the better of me. I asked him, "Why have you been ignoring me?"

He looked full of guilt and he said, "I know, I've been a jerk."

"Yeah you have."

"I'm just mad that I'm tied up and you're not. This rope is digging into my skin and into my scar, and I feel like you can just do whatever you want. You should have left by now."

"You are mad because York tied you up and not me?" I glared at him. I knew it. "You shouldn't be so quick to assume that York didn't do anything to me. If only you knew."

"Knew what?" he asked me.

I stole another look towards York to make sure he was still asleep and a long snore proved he was. I took a deep breath and explained to Carter everything York told me. I explained to him about how if I were to leave, York would set off a bomb that was hooked into that rope tied around his ankles.

"Well, why don't we just leave together?" Carter asked.

I told Carter how if I get too far away from York even if I'm still right next to Carter, York would know because of his censor and then continued to explain how he would set off another bomb.

Carter pondered this. "I feel horrible, Ana," he confessed. "This whole time I've been ticked because I had a rope tied around me. But, you had to know that my life is in your hands and if he ever became really angry he could just blow us up anyways! This guy is even crazier than I thought! Did you see all the weapons he has? And now I find out he has a bomb too? We have to find a way to get away from him."

"I know. But you can't act like you know about this. You have to act like you're still ticked off about being tied up and I'm not."

"Okay, I can do that."

"I know you can," I laughed with him, "now let me see your ankle."

He lifted his legs onto my lap and I tugged at the rope. It was tied so tight I could barely fit my hand under it. It was leaving scars on his ankles and when I looked at his right leg, I could see his older scar for the first time up-close. It was becoming severely inflamed where the rope was rubbing it.

"You've probably been wondering how I got my scar," he said. I took my eyes off it and realized I had been staring at it too long. I nodded my head yes and waited to see what he would say about his scar. I wondered why Carter had chosen now to reveal his secret but the thoughts didn't last very long. I was too anxious to hear the story to worry about why it was being told. The fire crackled on the wood and I stood up to put another log on. It snapped and popped as the flames danced over the new logs.

Carter stared into the fire and after several moments he took a deep breath and closed his eyes. "After my dad disappeared, I tried to carry on life as normal as I could. For the next two months, I hunted, gathered, and farmed a small garden. I scavenged in other people's houses around town and I waited for him. He never showed up. One day I decided I would wait one more week and then I was going to leave. I was going look for him, or any other people who could help me.

"Three days later, in the middle of the night, I was awoken by a sound. It was a harsh snarl right outside my bedroom window. I began to sit up in bed but then all of a sudden the window glass shattered all over me. Before I could even try to get out of bed and shake the glass off I was knocked over. This massive shape leaned over me, breathing hot air into my face and focusing on me with these bright, red eyes. This beast jumped on me and knocked me onto the floor. I tried to push him off, but he was too strong. I kicked him, but my leg got caught on his claw. He was trying to bat my leg away and his claws were too sharp. It dug into my leg and when I pulled away, it cut me all the way up to my thigh."

I gasped, shuttered, and closed my eyes imagining this.

"I was screaming from the pain and blood was gushing from my leg. He bit down on my shoulder then, and dragged out through the door way. I've still got that scar too."

He lifted up his shirt and turned around. On the back of his shoulder reaching to the front was a large row of bite marks which had healed and scarred over. He put his shirt back down and turned back to face me.

"So when this beast was dragging me out of my house he pulled me over all the window glass, and my hand caught of a large shard. Ignoring the pain I reached over and sliced it down his face until he let go of my shoulder. He howled so loud the entire house shook. I stood up on my good leg and attacked his face again. I sliced open his ear and his cheek. I knew I needed to get underneath him though. My dad had mentioned that his week point was his belly so I knew if I could just get the glass there, it could all be over.

"Using the glass on his face had infuriated the beast though, and he roared even louder than before. He lunged at me and I fell back on the floor, my head landing on the ground and every last breath was knocked out of me. He clawed at my chest and stood on my bad shoulder, but luckily not the shoulder that was holding the glass. I quickly jabbed the glass shard into his stomach and tugged it towards me, hard.

"Blood splattered all over my face and clothes and I was gasping for air. The beast jumped off me and went berserk. He thrashed around my room until he finally found the window. Leaping out of the whole, his massive size broke part of the wall and he disappeared.

"He was gone. I had beaten him. As I gasped for air I wanted to just lie on the floor and relax for hours but I knew I couldn't. I had to get some bandages on my leg and shoulder. I knew that if I didn't then I would bleed out so I quickly took off my shirt and tied it around my shin. Then I dragged myself to my closet and pulled another shirt down. I ripped off what was left of my pajama pants and tied the second shirt around my knee and thigh. It was hard to wrap my shoulder but eventually I was able to get a shirt around it. My hands were cut from holding the glass so I wrapped them too. Then I blacked out.

"I woke up sometime later, the sun in the sky, and I knew I had to clean the cuts. I crawled to the bathroom and found some alcohol to pour over the wounds which stung so badly, I have to admit I might have cried. And I re-wrapped them and put duct tape over the shirts to keep them in place.

"I spent the rest of the month healing and eating all the canned foods I had left. I built a crutch out of sticks in my back yard to help me move around, attempting to do everything I normally did. It seemed to take years for my wounds to heal, but at the end of the month, I left. I've been wandering around ever since." He stopped and took a deep breath.

"Have you ever told anybody that story before?" I asked.

He shook his head no. "The only people on the road I met were crazies who tried to mug me."

"I'm so sorry," I whispered. "Wait, is that the thing you think took Logan?"

"It's okay, but don't worry about it. You need some rest. Go to sleep and we can talk in the morning," he said.

"But —"

"Come on, Ana. We can talk some other time."

Nodding my head I left him, thinking about what he had shared with me and knowing he was probably thinking about what I told him too.

CHAPTER 25

LOGAN

SITTING NEXT TO me, there was a girl. She was lying on her side, unconscious. She had straight blonde hair that reached just above her waist and was wearing a pink t-shirt and blue jean shorts. She had a long cut up her leg like mine and also scrapes on her arms. Her leg was bleeding so much I was afraid she might die of blood loss so I pulled the rest of my shirt off and tore it into pieces, gently wrapping them around her leg. I was going to dip the shreds of cloth into my bucket of water and tie them around her leg, but I ran out of water.

All of a sudden I heard a growl. I looked up and to find beast hovering over me. He picked up the bucket in his mouth and trotted away. I looked over this girl and decided to start stanching the blood anyways. I was wrapping the final two pieces of my shirt around her left shin when I heard a crunch. I turned around and trotting towards us was the beast with the bucket in its mouth, water sloshing out of the sides. It set down the bucket and backed up into the smoke until I couldn't see anything but its bright red eyes watching us.

I unwrapped the bandages from her leg and poured water from the bucket onto them and onto the wound itself. The bucket was full and I wondered where it got the water from, but more importantly how it knew I needed the water. Pretty soon I had her whole leg wrapped up and the blood stopped gushing.

I wasn't sure what I was supposed to do to help her wake up, but I decided that maybe she needed a drink of water. I scooped up some water in my hands and dribbled it into her mouth. I only let a few drops into her mouth because if this didn't wake her up, there was a possibility she could have drowned. Plus I didn't want to waste any of it.

I stared at her for a minute and nothing happened. I scooped out a drink of water for myself and realized I was beyond parched. I was also famished, but there was nothing I could do about that. All of a sudden I saw her twitch. I was going to get another drink, but I dropped my hands to my sides and I watched her instead. Sure enough she moved her head to the side and started coughing. I lifted up her head a little and helped her sit up. She sat fully upright and stared at me. Then she looked down at her leg, pain mixing with the confusion on her face, and she looked around.

"Where am I?" she asked.

"Don't know myself," I replied. But I stuck out my hand. "I'm Logan."

"Maddie."

CHAPTER 26

CARTER

"HOW MUCH FARTHER are we going to walk today?" I complained. "Shut up, boy!" York said. "We've only been walking for six hours. We can go farther." He pulled out a map. "Hm, we have about two more miles and we reach Ohio."

"Why do you want to go to Ohio anyways? There's nothing there." I asked. Ana stayed silent.

"Oh, I don't plan on staying in Ohio; I plan on going all the way to Washington D.C."

"Wasn't Washington D.C. obliterated?" I asked.

He grunted. "Yep."

I was puzzled. "Then why do you want to go there?"

"That's where everyone with any sense is. The remainder of the US Army is there with shelter, food, and they are accepting any and all volunteers to join the army. I want in."

"Huh?" I asked, confused on his motives to bring us with him to join the army.

"I'm joining the army."

"I heard that much, but why are we here?" I asked.

He paused for a fraction of a second, trying to cover it and said, "I just want some company for my journey there."

"What!"

"Shut up, boy! And welcome to Ohio." York spread his arms out wide and we stared at the open road ahead of us. Besides a beat up state sign next to us, nothing pertaining to the scenery had changed.

We continued walking in silence. We made it about ten miles into Ohio. When the day was over we built a fire and ate some of my canned beans. Soon York was fast asleep and snoring away.

Ana was sitting next to me and once we were sure York was sound asleep we started whispering. "Ana, I think York is lying."

"About what?" she asked.

"When we were walking today York said he was going all the way to Washington D.C. to join the army. And the only reason we are here is to keep him company."

"Obviously!" Ana whispered angrily. "Something's not right. There are three stories here. One is that he kidnapped us and is using us to get him food and use all of our supplies. Two is that we are here keeping him company so he can join the army. And three is a reason unknown to us. Now, which one is most believable?"

I instantly knew which one was the truth, and the look Ana gave me confirms that she believed it as well. York was hiding something from us. But what?

"What should we do?" Ana asked.

"I don't know, but I know I'm sick of him, and we have to get out of here."

"I know. He's starting to drive me crazy, what with his stench and bad attitude. Also, he's just plain annoying."

"Ana, York seems to like you more than me. You need to find out if this rope really has a bomb inside it." I held up my tied hands.

"Yeah, it's pretty obvious he doesn't like you very much." Ana chuckled quietly. "Maybe if you would quit complaining all the time!" I pushed her gently and she pushed me back. Then in all seriousness she said, "We'll figure out a plan to get out of here, and to get away from him." Simultaneously we leaned back and looked up to the stars for guidance. Even with everything we had been through, they still brought peace. I didn't know how much time had passed when I realized that Ana was breathing deeply and sound asleep. I closed my eyes and tried to relax as well, but when a could breeze brought her closer to me, unconsciously pressing against me for warmth, my heart rate quickened uncontrollably and I knew that sleep would not be accompanying me any time soon.

CHAPTER 27

ANA

I WINKED AT CARTER and ran ahead to York. "York!" I called.

"What do you want," he grunted, not even bothering to look in my direction.

"I just want to talk to you."

"About what," he said again in an annoyed voice.

"Carter told me we are all going to Washington D.C. Do you really want to join the army? And how do you even know there is still an army. Based on everything I've heard, our national government is completely destroyed and that's why we are all living like we are pioneers and are surviving on canned goods and whatever scraps of animals we can find." I rambled on for a while longer.

"Well, little miss, you have a point there. I want to be in the army. I've always wanted to be, but my parents never wanted me too. And besides, until now there wasn't a reason to join. But, I'm 31 years old. I deserve to do whatever I want and join the army." After some consideration he said, "I think there is still an army. We have to have something out there at least trying to defend our nation. Or, what used to be our nation. I wonder if people even call us The United States of America. We certainly aren't united."

He stared off ahead, lost in his own thoughts. For a second, he almost seemed like a normal guy. It was unnerving so I snapped my fingers in front of his face to get his attention until he jumps and turned his head back to me.

"So, when did you learn to set bombs?" I asked him.

"Well, let's see. I took an interest in bombs about the same time I took an interest in joining the army." He scratched his head for a minute, "That's got to be about fourteen years ago now."

"That's a long time," I said, shocked.

"Yep, well I'm tired of talking little miss. Why don't you go back to Carter and bug him some more."

"You called him Carter," I smirked. He glared at me as he continued walking, so I stopped and waited for Carter to catch up with me instead.

"So?" he asked. "What'd he say?"

"Well, you were right about him joining the army."

"Yeah, but what about the bombs?"

"I think those really are bombs. He told me he's been working on how to build bombs for fourteen years!"

Carter's jaw dropped a little bit and he shook his head slowly. "Well, we need to come up with a plan. And we need to figure it out now." His voice had a serious depth to it and he lowered it even more. "I plan on leaving tonight."

CHAPTER 28

LOGAN

"Hi, Maddie."

"Hi, Logan. My leg is killing me! Did you wrap it up?" She inspected her leg and gingerly attempted to move it, but the pained look that distorted her face showed me that she wouldn't be going anywhere anytime soon.

"Yeah, do you need some water?" She nodded her head yes. I picked up the bucket and I set it down beside her so she could reach her hands in and take a few drinks.

"Is there any food?" She asked. "I'm starving! I haven't eaten in... two days, I think... How long was I out?"

"Since you were brought here, only about a half hour. I don't know how long you were passed out before that."

"It was horrible, Logan. I was putting logs on the fire and all of a sudden the window next to me shattered and I was knocked down. This huge black dog-wolf thing sliced me up my leg and bit my arm. It grabbed me and it dragged me out of the house. On the way out I hit my head on the wall and that's the last thing I remember since I blacked out. My arm is still bleeding. Do you have anything else to wrap it up with?"

I didn't but I looked around anyways. "No, but you can just tear the bottom of your shirt off and it will do just fine."

Following my advice she ripped off the bottom hem line and handed it to me so I could soak it in water. Then she raised her arm and I saw a horrible gash mark. I wonder how I didn't see that before when I was cleaning up her leg. The blood had mostly stopped flowing, but once I finished tying the shirt around her arms, the shirt stopped the remaining blood flow.

"Thank you," Maddie said even though I could tell it must have hurt.

"Of course," I said and I looked into her eyes. They were big, bright, blue and I realized for the first time that she looked scared.

CHAPTER 29

CARTER

"A NA!" I WHISPERED. She walked over to me and plopped down. "You know what to do?"

She saluted me and said, "Ay-ay Captain!"

"We aren't on a ship you know." She shoved my arm and knocked me over, but because I was tied up I couldn't stop myself and I landed on my side. Pushing myself up was harder than I thought it would be, and Ana amused herself by watching me struggle. After laughing and deciding to help pull me upright again, she stood up and sauntered over to York.

"Hi, York!" I heard her say in a chipper voice. She was good at acting innocent, and I hoped that York bought it. Then her voice became quieter and they argued back and forth a few times. After a few minutes she reached behind York and grabbed my backpack. She rummaged through it and a shocked expression came over her face. She held up my bottle of scotch and I could see York's eyes light up. He opened it and instantly started drinking it.

Ana backed away and returned to me. As she passed she said, "Right on track," and she sat down a few feet away from me and smiled. We both watched York finish the scotch and soon he was lying on his back singing words we could not understand. We waited and an hour later he was passed out.

"Come on, Carter," Ana said as she walked past me. She kneeled down next to York and slapped his cheek. He didn't even move. "Yes!" She raised her fist in the air and she grabbed her backpack. I snatched mine as well and searched it. I pulled out two cans of food, my clothes, everything else I packed, but no censor.

"Ana, search your backpack. The censor thing isn't in mine!"

"What? It's not in there?" She rummaged through her backpack and came out with nothing. "It's not in mine! Where is it?"

"Check his pants," I suggested.

"What!" She yelled. "I don't think so! You check his pants."

I kneeled down next to him and searched through his pockets. I didn't find anything. "Where is it?"

I stood up and looked around frantically. Ana walked up behind me and tapped my shoulder. I turned around and she was smiling. In her hand was York's jacket. She reached into one of the pockets and waved the censor in front of my face.

"Looking for something?" She taunted me. She turned around and walked away. I followed her and once we were a few feet away from York she whipped out her pocket knife. "Let's cut these babies off!" She started sawing into the ropes and once they were cut all the way through, the censor in my hand started beeping like crazy. "He wasn't kidding!" Ana yelled.

We both flip the rope over and over looking for a way to shut it off but all of a sudden we both hear a grunt. We froze and looked over at the fire. York was trying to stand up. He looked over at us and saw the censor, his eyes flaring up and he stumbled towards us.

Not sure how much time was left before the bomb would explode Ana grabbed my hands, throwing the censor behind her. "Come on! Hurry up!" We ran through the forest until we reached the highway. We stopped and turned around. Sticks were crunching behind us and feet were stomping. Then we hear a thump and a curse. He must have hit a tree.

"Come back here you kids!" He yelled. We heard another thump and another curse word, but we didn't hear him get back up and chase after us. Ana and I took off down the road.

Moments later, we heard the small explosion.

CHAPTER 30

ANA

CARTER AND I raced off down the road with our flashlights shining. We knew we had to get as far as we could because York could follow us in the morning if he wasn't too badly harmed. After a few miles we stopped and took a break. I lifted my leg and Carter grabbed it. I shined my flashlight on the censor which was still strapped to my leg so we could inspect how to get it off.

"I'm not sure how this thing works. We need to wait until morning so I can see it better. Let's keep going," Carter said.

We raced off down the road for about five miles before we called it quits. Hopefully if York was drunk enough and burned enough he wouldn't be able to start looking for us early in the morning. We decided instead to camp out on the edge of the road again. Judging by the moon it was about two a.m.

We were both exhausted from walking all day, staying up until York passed out drunk, and running the extra miles. We both fell asleep almost instantly.

A beeping noise roused me from my dreamless sleep. It was morning, the sun was partly in the sky and it took a moment for me to realize the beeping was coming from my backpack. I shook Carter with my right hand and continued pulling things out of my backpack. But then my back pack was empty and I saw nothing that could make a beeping noise. But I still heard it. Carter finally opened his eyes and said something so groggily I couldn't understand him. I shushed him and listened carefully. The beeping was coming from the pile of gear on the ground. I rummaged through it frantically and narrowed the search down to my small pile of clothes. Finally I unwrapped my t-shirt and inside were the two VCR's. One screen was on and flashing. I pressed the power button and almost screamed.

York's face was smiling wide at me. "Hi there, Sunshine."

I was speechless and Carter scooted next to me and an expression of shock came over his face also.

"There you are, Carter. You two pulled off a real sneaky stunt back there yesterday. I have to hand it to you though, that was pretty genius. But don't think you won't get away with it. You didn't really think you were only with me for company, right? Why would I set a perfect trap with the model pack alongside the road just for company?" he laughed and shook his head. "What, cat got your tongue?"

Cater and I stammered incomprehensible words.

"That's what I thought." Then he leaned in really close to the camera. "You can run, and you can hide, but I'm coming after you. There's no escape." The VCR shut off.

I looked at Carter with a look of horror on my face. "We have to get as far away as we can."

"Agreed."

Carter and I threw everything back into my backpack and we set off down the road. "Was that creepy or what?"

"Very creepy. Ana, this guy could be seriously messed up, you know, up there," he pointed to his head.

"I know which makes it all worse. We could be in serious trouble."

"I know, let's go. We have to get out of Ohio."

Chapter 31

Logan

MADDIE WAS TIRED from her long day and all of her blood loss. I told her to go to sleep and that I would keep watch in case anything happened, to put her at ease. She took off her tennis shoes and rested her head back on them. Soon she was out like a light and it became dark.

When the wind was blowing through my hair and my clothes I realized how much I stunk. I needed a shower with ten bars of soap. I looked up at the dark blanket that was the night sky. Usually the smoke was so thick I couldn't see the stars properly, instead only a hazy light trying to peek through the smoke was noticeable. That night was different though. As I looked up, I could see the stars clearly. The smoke was gone.

Seeing the stars affected me. It gave me a sense of hope. A sense that we would escape, and that I would find Ana. I just needed to wait for the right time. I needed to wait for my leg to heal and I had to help Maddie. What we both needed right then was food. If we didn't have food then there is no way we would get better and leave.

I took my gaze off the stars above me and turned to my right. I saw those bright, red eyes watching me and I knew I couldn't get out until that beast was gone.

CHAPTER 32

CARTER

I LOOKED AT ANA and saw that she was weary and panting. "Ana, we can't go on like this. We have to stop and hunt or eat a can of food. We are going to tire ourselves to death. We've been walking and jogging for three hours and we haven't eaten in like 35 hours."

Ana slowed to a walk, and then stopped all together. Her hands were on her sides and she bent over. "Hold on!" She yelled and ran to the side of the road, quickly looking away when I realized she was gagging and about to vomit the little bit that was left in her stomach over the railing. When she finished she asked me for a water bottle to rinse her mouth out.

While she was cleaning out her mouth I started collecting wood and by the time she was finished I had a fire going. I held up a can of green beans and a can of tomato soup. "Which one do you want to eat tonight?" I asked as she turned around. I could tell she was still a little embarrassed from throwing up so I avoided the subject and just stayed focused on dinner. She pointed to the green beans and I agreed with her. It was probably better to get some actual food in our stomachs – not just liquids. I set it next to the fire so it could cook.

While we were waiting Ana sat next to me on the ground and wrapped her knees up, resting her chin on them. "Sometimes this all just feels so hopeless." She finally said. She looked tired. And not just the feeling of being tired but her entirety seemed worn out. "I mean, we are going to Indianapolis in search of shelter which may or may not be there while York is hunting us down, along with who knows what else, and we are not a single step closer to finding my brother. Running until I puke, practically starving ourselves, what is the point anymore?"

"It's because there *is* hope," I said. "If there wasn't the possibility that a safe shelter might actually exist and people might still be managing to survive then I think we would all go crazy trying to accept the fact that we are all alone. It may be false hope, but it's still hope and that counts for something."

"But what if it is false hope? What if it's all just a lie in the end?"

"Because even false hope is strength." I sat, staring into the fire and gently poking the logs with a stick as we both became quiet, settling into the comfortable silence with most often accompanied our meals.

The next morning Ana and I were refreshed and ready to go. I looked out into the distance searching for any kind of hope to hang on to. We set out at a walk. While we were walking we saw a sign that said Greenville, Ohio. I pulled out an electronic pocket map and punched in the city. The screen lit up, indicating that the nearest main road was route 127.

I told Ana, "We have to walk a few miles east and we will get on route 127. Then we follow it south and it intersects with highway 70 that will lead us straight to Indianapolis."

"Finally! Come on!" She sauntered down the road and I ran to catch up with her. For the first time in a long time I could see a genuine smile on her face.

"A penny for your thoughts," I asked Ana.

"I was just thinking that the sooner we get to Indianapolis, the sooner we can find Logan. I can't wait for when I'm going to see him, I miss him so much! I've been with Logan my whole life and if it weren't for him I probably wouldn't have survived and he's out somewhere all alone with that beast!"

"You know we will try to find your brother and help him when the time is right, don't you?"

"You're right, I just wish that time was closer," she said.

"I know you feel horrible about Logan, but, Ana, there's nothing you could do. We are going to get him back. I promise you. That's what we are here to do. No matter what crosses our path, we are going to go find Logan. Don't you forget that. He's alive and safe. I just know it. We are going to save him. Together." And a little bit of hope could be seen in the soft smile which slowly crept onto Ana's face.

CHAPTER 33

ANA

As Carter and I were walking we passed a forest. It looked fuller and lusher than the other woods we'd seen so far. "Carter, I know we just ate green beans this morning, but this might be our only chance to hunt for a while. Plus, we can't keep relying on canned food. I only have two cans left. Let's stop and hunt."

"That's exactly what I was thinking," Carter said, "And we can use these VCR's so we can split up and hunt. We might be able to catch more game that way too."

"Good idea. Let's put our stuff down here and make camp. This is our meeting spot for when we are done hunting. If I'm not back within… let's say two hours, call on me on the VCR and I'll do the same for you."

"Alright, sounds good. This is going to be fun!" Carter stalked off in one direction into the woods and I decided to go the opposite way. I trekked through the woods about three quarters of a mile. Then I found a small tree surrounded by shrubs and waited. My bow and arrow was poised at the ready and I watched and listened to my surroundings. I heard birds chirping but they were far off. Maybe they were close to where Carter was.

My legs became stiff and I started to shift when suddenly I heard a crunch. I looked to my left and focused, listening intently for another sound. Soon I saw a quail hopping through the small bushes next to me. It took one last hop and started to take air when I shot. The arrow hit directly into its heart and it fell back to the ground.

I jumped out of my tree and looked up to examine the sun. It had probably been close to two hours so I hurried back to the camp. On my way back I heard a roar and a scream. I heard a couple gun shots, then silence. The only other person here is Carter. I stopped dead in my tracks and whipped out my VCR. I called Carter and stared expectantly into the screen.

Nothing happened for the longest minute of my life. Then the screen lit up and Carter's face appeared. I knew something was wrong. There was blood in his blonde hair and there was a gash on his forehead that was dripping blood. "Carter!" I yelled.

"Ana…" he barely whispered it.

"Where are you?"

"I went about a mile west of our camp."

"I'm coming! Hold on!" I started sprinting as fast as I could and soon I was passing the camp and on my way to Carter.

CHAPTER 34

CARTER

I HEARD THRASHING IN the woods near me and I knew Ana would be here to help me soon. My arm was burning and the five deep gashes were streaming out blood. The bear was lying still on the ground in front of me. It took five shots and a busted arm to kill it. The thing was rabid; it came at me from behind and struck me when I was unprepared. It had foam forming at its mouth and it had cuts and scars covering its body. There were many places where large tufts of hair had been pulled out. This wasn't good.

All of a sudden Ana burst through the trees sweating and panting. "Carter! What happened to you?"

I pointed at the bear and Ana became instantly horrified. When she saw my arm a look of disbelief came over her. She ran and kneeled at my side. "Carter!" She took a few breaths and closed her eyes, deep in thought. "Okay, we have to stop the blood flow." She looked around her and then focused on my chest. "We have to use your shirt." She cut off the sleeve on my damaged arm and then gently slid the shirt off over my head.

She tore the shirt apart and tried not to stare at me. Once my shirt was in about five different pieces she started wrapping it around my arm. Her small fingers caressed my arm so gingerly and the feel of her touch on my skin calmed me a little. Soon she had it all wrapped and let go of my arm.

"Can you walk?" She asked me. This was what I feared most. I was afraid that my blood loss is too much and I wouldn't be strong enough to walk a mile back to our campsite. I knew I had to try though. I let my bad arm hang limply at my side and I used my right arm to lift myself up. Ana grabbed my arm and helped me stand. I wobbled a little but stayed up.

I took a step and almost instantly fell to the ground. Ana caught me and held me steady. "Stand still," she instructed. She put on her backpack and I saw a quail tied to it. Then she wrapped my right arm around her shoulders. She was just the right height so her shoulder fit squarely into my side. She then proceeded to wrap one arm around my bare back and her touch sent tingles though my spine, despite the pain. I hoped she couldn't tell. Her other hand was holding mine in place around her shoulders.

"Lean on me," she instructed. She had a look of determination upon her face as we began.

We start walking and I felt horrible. Ana was using all her strength to keep me upright and walking. By the time we were half way to camp Ana was panting; a line a sweat forming along her forehead and I was so dizzy I could see stars. "Break," I whispered and Ana stopped walking. She sat next to me and we leaned against a tree. She pulled out a water bottle and took a drink then offered it to me.

Water tasted so good and I almost drank it all. I had to stop myself after a few gulps because this was all the water she had left. After ten minutes or so Ana hauled herself up and gently pulled me up after her. She wrapped her arm around me tightly once again and held me in place. I placed my arm on her shoulders and held her hand.

We walked step by step ever so slowly and finally we made it back to camp. We pushed though a few low lying branches and stepped into the small clearing. What we see shocked us.

Going through my backpack was a boy.

CHAPTER 35

ANA

I STARED IN DISBELIEF. There was a boy, around our age with short brown hair, digging through Carter's backpack. He was very skinny and if he took off his shirt I bet I could have seen his ribs. I pulled out my bow and set it at the ready. "Who are you!" I yelled. The boy jumped and turned around. He noticed my bow right away and walked backwards, tripping over Carter's backpack and falling onto the ground. I helped Carter sit down and then I walked over to him. "I said who are you?" I pointed the arrow right in his face.

"M-marcus!" He stammered.

"So, Marcus, what are you doing here at our camp, digging through Carter's backpack."

"Um... um..." He was at a loss for words.

"Get up." I move the bow away from his face but kept it pointed at him. He slowly rose and we both stared at each other expectantly. I spoke first. "What should I do with you? I can't just let you get away with this, but I can't kill you. It would be a waste." He started to move backwards away from me at that comment. "Hold up! That doesn't mean I can't just injure you."

I looked over at Carter who was watching silently as the scene unfolded. I noticed the scars on his wrists from York's ropes and I got an idea. "I know what we can do with you." I reached into my backpack and pulled out one of the ropes York had tied Carter up with. I used it for holding game and securing my water bottles in place. "Hold out your wrists." I commanded.

He does as he was told and I was about to tie them together when Carter stopped me. "Ana, wait."

"What!" I snap at him, not daring to take my eyes off Marcus.

"We can't tie him up. If we do we will be just like York."

This stunned me and I lowered my bow to my side and unload it. "I know," I whispered.

Marcus stared at Carter in confusion, but after a while a smile snuck onto his face. He walked over and stood in front of Carter. "Wow. What happened to you?"

"I got attacked by a bear. Lost a lot of blood."

"I can tell you are as pale as a ghost, man."

Carter chuckled feebly. "I feel like a ghost. I don't know how much longer I can go without resting."

"Do you need help making a fire?" Marcus asked.

"Yeah, that'd be great," Carter showed a weak smile.

"Wait a minute!" I exclaimed. "Why would we let him join us? I can get a fire going on my own very easily and in case you didn't remember, a minute ago that boy was trying to steal all of your stuff!"

Carter eyed Marcus suspiciously. "Why should I let you stay?"

"Well, I'm pretty cute, huh?" He turned in my direction and raised his eyebrows a few times, proceeding to wink at me.

"Oh, get over yourself," I snapped at Marcus.

"Well, Marcus," Carter said, "why don't you go collect some wood while I talk to Ana for a little while?"

Marcus smiled at me. "Sounds good. I'll be back later." He set out into the forest and once he was out of sight Carter turned to me.

"Are you mean to everyone you meet?"

"I don't know what you're talking about," I replied stiffly.

"Oh," Carter scoffed, "You don't remember when we first met? It was a little like what's happening right now, bow and everything."

"If I can remember right, you were trying to steal my backpack!" I whispered harshly.

"Hm, if I remember correctly, you're backpack was in plain sight and I was just trying to figure out who it belonged to. Then you came along and we've had a great relationship so far if you ask me."

"A great relationship! First of all, we aren't dating –"

"Never said we were dating," he interrupted.

"–and in case you forgot, we got chased out of my house by some scientists who have gone berserk, we got attacked by a wild lady, kidnapped by York who is still out there somewhere, and finally got away when a bear attacked you! And now this boy is trying to steal our stuff! I don't think we've had the best relationship here, or the best of luck."

"Speaking of getting attacked by a bear, can you get my first aid box out of my backpack?" Carter asked me.

"I don't know. Can I? Or did Marcus steal it!" I huffed and trudged over to the backpack, pulling out the first aid kit and handing it to Carter. He searched around, but didn't find what he was looking for and placed it back on the ground again.

"Now," Carter started again, "I think Marcus was only trying to look out for himself. We really shouldn't have left my backpack just lying here at the campsite."

"How were we supposed to know there were this many people not in Indianapolis? I thought everyone had left."

"We've only seen three people as far as I can remember and besides, it doesn't really matter does it?" Carter asked. "I say we let him stay. Yes, he's another mouth to feed and from what I can tell he didn't come with much, but he's also another hunter, and he's another person to protect us if something happens again like the whole York situation."

I thought this over. He had a point. Finally, I agreed. "We are not going to let him talk us into going any place besides Indy. He can stay. But on one condition."

"What?" Carter asked.

"I'm in charge from here on out."

CHAPTER 36

LOGAN

MADDIE WAS GETTING stronger every day. Her leg had finally stopped bleeding and she wasn't as tired. She was becoming aware of her surroundings and could see the beast for the first time. It was carrying a bucket of food that contained bread and a few apples. I didn't know where the beast found the apples since I had assumed all of the apple trees probably died in the bombing, but I was happy to have them. So, as the beast came nearer with the bucket I stayed as still as I could, trying to stay calm, but it was obvious Maddie was horrified. Maddie slid next to me and gripped my hand.

"It's okay," I whispered.

She just shook her head and kept her eyes on the beast. "That thing still horrifies me even if it is bringing me food."

"It was violent when found me," I said, "but since I've been here it hasn't ever tried to do anything with me. It knows when I am hungry and thirsty. But, Maddie, something's wrong with it."

"What do you mean?" She stared at me quizzically.

"It can talk."

She let out a tiny giggle and clasped her hand over her mouth, shocked that she could laugh when she was so nervous just seconds before. "You're kidding."

"I'm serious." I looked her straight in the eye. "When I was first here, jeez I can't even remember how long ago that was, but when it first brought me here, it looked me straight in the eyes with those bright, red, menacing eyes of its and it snarled 'stay put.'"

"What?"

"I'm dead serious, Maddie. This thing isn't just some animal. There's something else to it. I just haven't been able to study it close enough to figure it out. One thing I'm pretty sure of though, is that someone told it to bring us here."

"Someone told that thing to bring us here?"

"Yes, why else would they pick us out of everybody else in the world. It didn't get my sister, Ana. She was in the same house as me the night the beast showed up. It brought us here to this dump, I don't even know where we are, but it brought us here for a reason."

"Wait. You don't know where we are?"

I shook my head no.

"We're in Gary," she said.

"What? How do you know that?"

"Look around us. They turned this city into a dump thirty years ago. Where are you from that you didn't know this?"

"I'm from Valparaiso, but wait. They? They who?"

"The scientists."

CHAPTER 37

CARTER

THAT NIGHT MARCUS and I talked after Ana fell asleep. He told me he was from Toledo. He'd been traveling around Ohio trying to find any stragglers who hadn't gone to Columbus yet. Besides crazy people, we were the only kids he'd found. He met a couple adults who were traveling down to Columbus, but most of Ohio was already deserted. He did find though, a caravan of mostly hippies who were traveling west. He didn't bother with them though, said they were too odd.

"It's not like one of the big states like California or New York. Nobody wants to stay here. They all want to go somewhere where there is leadership. Where there is organization. All this," Marcus waved his arms around, "it's too much for most people. In fact, if I hadn't found you two I probably would have decided it was time to leave and head for Columbus. It's getting to be too much for me anymore. I'm out of food and have to hunt. I've never really been into hunting sports, but it sure would have helped. How was I supposed to know I'd need to rely on hunting to eat? How did any of us know?

"Everyone says we lost most of our population from the bombing, which is probably true. But if you ask me, a big chunk of losses were from people who couldn't hunt and who couldn't find any more food that wasn't spoiled rotten. The city slickers probably died from starvation."

I nodded my head in agreement. I'd always been crafty with a rifle, but I had to give it to Ana. It took a lot of skill to learn how to bow hunt. I didn't know where she learned. In fact, I realized there was a lot about her that I didn't know. She probably learned to bow hunt from her dad or her brother.

I leaned against the tree and took a deep breath.

"Hey man, do you feel alright? You don't look so good."

"I don't feel so hot," I said. "It's probably from the blood loss. I need to sleep. I'll talk to you in the morning."

Marcus nodded and stared back at the fire as I laid down in my sleeping bag. Soon I was sound asleep.

Splash! I popped open my eye and my hand darted to my nose. I looked up at the sky and a rain drop hit me square in the eye. Though my arm stung I felt much better after resting. I was starving though. I ate last night but it wasn't enough. I looked around and next to me I saw a small piece of the quail next to me and I snatched it up. It was gone in two bites but it satisfied me. I knew Ana must have torn this piece out of her own food just so I could eat.

I wondered if she'd ever considered becoming a doctor. Or, I guess if she had considered it. I doubted she could go to medical school now. She seemed to know just what to do whenever something happened. I was always too freaked out to do anything. I froze up at the sight of blood. Ana was strong. She really was. To have been abandoned by her parents and survived on her own with Logan was amazing. Then to set out in search of him without knowing where exactly he had gone was an even bigger sense of courage – or stupidity I guess. I decided to pay more attention to her and try to be like her. I guess it was a good thing she was in charge. She needed it.

The rain started drizzling and Ana woke up. She paused, then sat up and looked at me. And it was not the welcoming glance I had suspected. It was a cold, hard glare. She pointed across the smoking remains of the fire and noticed what she was looking at – nothing. Marcus was gone. Ana stood up and stormed over to me.

"Where is he?" She questioned me.

I put up my hands in defense.

"Your backpack is gone too! Carter I knew we shouldn't have let him stay the night with us! He ate some of our food then waited until we were asleep and then he took off without us and stole your backpack! I knew we shouldn't have trusted him!"

"Trusted who?" We both heard. There were approaching footsteps, Ana's eyes flared and I turned around to see Marcus striding towards us with a pile of wood in his hands and Carter's backpack strapped tightly his back. "I could tell it was going to rain so I figured it would be better to have some dry fire wood with us so once the rain is over it will be easy to light. I took Carter's backpack because there are weapons in there and based on his arm, there could be some real threats in that wood."

"So you took all of our weapons and left us unprotected?" Ana questioned.

"No, you have your bow and Carter has his handgun… you do have your gun, right Carter?"

I nodded my head. My gun was still hooked to my pant loop. Ana fumed and returned to her sleeping bag under the shelter of the forest canopy, hiding and sulking from the rain.

"Come on man, you didn't think I'd take off on you, now do you?" Marcus asked me.

"Nah, I trust you. It's Ana who doesn't trust you."

"Yeah, what's her deal?" He asked me.

"Hard times. She's had some really hard times."

"We all have, man."

"I know, I know. She'll come around. Just takes some time for her to warm up to people. Don't sweat it. She doesn't hate you too much."

Marcus grins, "Thanks man, she's a pretty one." He stared at Ana for a few moments before settling down to rest. He took one last glance at Ana then closed his eyes. This bothered me. I decided I was going to watch out for him and keep him away from Ana. *Am I jealous?*

CHAPTER 38

ANA

*M*ARCUS IS SO *irritating! He's so smug and rude. I can't believe him.* I had to calm down and not think about that though. I had other things that were more important. He was just a distraction. If I ignored him and worried about what was really important I'd be fine.

The most important thing right now was Carter. He seemed fine, but he might have been sick. I didn't know if that bear had any diseases but based on the state of this country, I wouldn't have been shocked if even diseases were topsy-turvy. He seemed fine but I would have to remember to watch for any signs that something was wrong. I didn't even know what any of the signs might have been. I was a horrible doctor, but oh well, I was now in charge of this brigade and what I said goes.

We were wasting away this day by just sitting at camp. My mind kept wandering to Marcus, food, water, and a bath. I would have given anything for a bath. I probably stunk, but I didn't think about it. Making something real in your mind made you acknowledge your own stink as well as others'.

The rain was seeping through the leaves and every once in a while I felt a drop hit me, but for the most part being under the forest canopy wasn't too bad. My sleeping bag was on the ground and getting wet from ground water though. Before we left, we would all have to wait a few hours for our sleeping bags to dry. That meant another night here and a few hours in the morning if the rain let up soon. If not, we were looking at two more days. I didn't know if I could take it any longer. I was too restless.

I stared around the camp and saw Marcus sleeping and Carter thinking. I picked up my bow and stood up. I walked through the middle of camp, and as I passed Carter I told him I was going hunting. I didn't know if the rain would help or hurt my chances of getting something, but I set out anyways. I had to get away from there. I had to get away from my thoughts.

I climbed into a small tree and cleared my mind. All other thoughts escaped and I focused my thoughts on hunting. I listened for bird calls and animal steps. After a few hours of nothing, I gave up and walked back to camp. Carter and Marcus were in the same positions except Marcus was awake. As I strolled in Marcus turned his gaze to me and smiled. "I was starting to get worried for a minute there. You were gone for a long time missy. Do we need to talk about this?" Marcus clicked his tongue and placed his hands on his hips, irritatingly tapping his foot on the ground.

I rolled my eyes and took a deep breath. All my stress that hunting had taken away came rushing back. I almost turned around and stalked back out but decided against it. The rain had finally stopped and there was still and hour or two or daylight left. The days were growing longer by a few minutes each day and in a month or two it would be light until nine o-clock.

Summer would make hunting easier because all the animals would be out grazing and the temperature wouldn't be so bad for sleeping. I lifted my sleeping bag up from the ground and hung it over a tree branch. Carter and Marcus noticed me and did the same. We all decided not to eat because I didn't get anything and we were almost completely out of canned food.

"Alright," I said. "Because the rain has stopped we can continue on. I'm tired of sitting here and doing nothing, so tomorrow we are heading out. Marcus, can you go find some long sticks for Carter? Bring a couple back so we can find one the right height and he can use it as a walking stick. Also, if you want to hunt while you are out go ahead. In the morning we need to eat something and if you don't catch anything we will have to have some peas, the last peas we will have for a long time. Carter, get some rest. I plan on leaving bright and early and walking all day. We lost a whole day of travel today because of the rain and Carter's arm. We have to make up for it."

Carter rested his head against some thick grass and closed his eyes while Marcus grabbed a gun and turned to the forest without a word. That went quite well I thought. I just hoped Carter would be strong enough to travel. The next day we would leave and we would be even closer to Indianapolis so we could get to Logan. Before it was too late.

CHAPTER 39

LOGAN

I LOOKED AT MADDIE with my jaw hanging open. "The scientists? They did this? The scientists at GFS? My parents work for them. They wouldn't leave me in here. If it was really them they would have rescued me a long time ago."

"Look, it may or may not be your parents working on this project. All I know is that those scientists created that thing. I don't know why or how or what our plan in this is, but they did it."

"How do you know all this?" I asked her.

"I don't think I should tell you right now. It's not a good time."

"Now is as good a time as ever."

She looked around her, and then looked up. "We should wait. I don't feel right telling you now."

She closed her mouth and looked around again. She was set on not saying anything now and I wasn't going to press the subject. As the rest of the day went on though, I couldn't get it out of my mind.

When the night sky came alive with stars, I turned to Maddie. "You have to tell me!"

"I can't. I don't think I should."

"I've been waiting all day and I need to know. You can't drop a bomb like you did and not tell me, now."

"I know, but I'm afraid they will hear."

"They?"

"The scientists. I don't know but they might have this place rigged with microphones."

"Why would they do that?"

"To see if we are going to escape or something. Like I said, I don't know the whole story, but I wouldn't put it past them to do that." She keeps looking around her like she's watching for something.

"How do you know this?"

She leaned in next to my ear and I could hear her breath on my neck. Ever so quietly she whispered into my ear. "I used to be one of them."

CHAPTER 40

CARTER

THE NIGHT WAS chilly and it was hard to sleep. By morning I was itching to eat and leave. I still had the chills and I knew some warm food and exercise would warm me up. I knew Ana said she wanted to walk all day, but I didn't know how long I could keep up. I didn't feel very well that morning. I felt even worse than I had the day before.

I tried to forget about it as I tried to roll up my sleeping bag and pack up. I couldn't get it tight enough though and the bag kept uncurling until Marcus helped me keep it together. None of the walking sticks Marcus brought me were as well designed and strong as my old stick, but I left it on the road when we were taken by York. I picked the sturdiest one. It would have to do. I didn't need it for my leg anymore but I was still feeling a little feeble from blood loss so I needed it to stay upright.

"Are you both ready?" Ana asked us.

I looked at Marcus and he looked back at me. "Yep," We said simultaneously.

"Let's get going. We're wasting daylight," Ana said as she turned and headed away from the rising sun, knowing it would eventually catch up to us. I shrugged my shoulders at Marcus and started walking and Marcus quickly followed suit.

It was almost May now, and as the sun peeked over the trees, I felt the effects of the oncoming heat. The sun's beams of light were directed right at me. Pretty soon I was sweating and I stopped everyone so I could take off my sweatshirt.

Ana looked annoyed that we had to stop, but I ignored it. Maybe she needed to get over herself a little bit. Just because I agreed she could be in charge of where we went from here on out didn't give her the right to boss us around and act superior. She was being awfully rude.

I shook my head and pulled my backpack up over my shoulders and Ana continued on in silence. By the end of the day I had finished my entire water bottle and I was still parched. My lips were cracked and my throat burned something fierce. I needed water. I decided not to say anything though because I'd already made Ana stop twice so I could go to the bathroom and take a breather.

All of a sudden Marcus came to a complete halt in front of me. I crashed into his back pack, practically causing me to fall to the ground. "Sorry!" I said, gingerly holding my arm and trying to hold myself upright.

"Sh! Listen, man!"

I closed my eyes and listened to the sounds around me. I thought I heard a faint trickling sound but I was not positive. Ana reassured me.

She yelled, "Water!"

"It's that way," Marcus pointed off to the left.

Ana dashed towards the small trees lining the road and Marcus took off after her. I attempted to run after them but my head felt really heavy, too heavy for my body and I had to take it slow and breathe. A few hundred feet off the road was a stream. It was not too big, maybe fifteen feet across at its widest point, but it looked cool and refreshing. I dipped my hands in and splashed my face. The water droplets slid down my eyelids onto my cheeks and continued sliding down my neck. It felt more than wonderful to wipe away to dirt and the sweat.

I noticed Ana and Marcus doing the same and I took off my backpack. I dropped it on the bank of the river and sat down next to it. I pulled off my shoes and socks and rolled up my pant legs. I waded into the water and right away it was all the way up to my shins and then my knees. "I could go for a bath, what about you two?"

"Definitely," the said simultaneously.

"Carter, you can go first," Ana said, "And Marcus can go next. I don't mind being last. I saved an empty can so I'll collect water in it and boil it over the fire to get rid of any germs. Once you're done it should be heated enough so I can get another can going. While we are here we should all do wash also. I don't know about you two, but I'm tired of wearing dirty clothes!"

"Amen to that, sister," Marcus praised. "Carter, we will give you some privacy and make camp a couple yards that way. See you later, man." Marcus trudged off and Ana followed, leaving me to my peace.

Slowly I undressed and waded all the way into the water. I ducked under and the water rushed over my skin, instantly cooling me down. The water covered me and for a few moments I was suspended, weightless, in the water, and when I resurfaced I felt instantly better. I swam back to shore and pulled out the tiny bar of soap I packed with me and scrubbed it all over my body. I'd never been so happy to have soap. I could literally peel off a layer of dirt from my good arm.

It took me a good twenty minutes before I was fully satisfied with washing and when I was done my skin felt raw. It needed it though. I ran the soap through my hair and ducked under the water again. I scrubbed my head vigorously and came up for air. My hair was getting long and shaggy which I kind of liked. It made me feel rugged. My facial hair was also starting to grow in which definitely made me feel tough.

When I got back to my backpack I realized I didn't have a towel. I decided to try and dry off with my sweatshirt and I pulled on my boxers. Before I went back to the fire to dry off the rest of the way I dunked all of my clothes in the river. I rung them out so they weren't dripping and headed back so Marcus could take his turn in the stream.

"Wait!" Ana yelled and she dashed for the stream.

"What's going on?" I asked Marcus.

"She needs more water to boil."

I nodded my head. "Got it."

"I'm heading down there whether she's still there or not. I'm ready to be clean again!"

"Trust me, it's a good feeling."

Marcus nodded farewell and sauntered towards the stream singing an old nursery song. "…splish splash I was taking a bath…"

I then realized I was shivering and stood next to the fire to warm up. All my clothes were soaked except my boxers. I hung the clothes on tree branches and prayed they would dry fast.

CHAPTER 41

ANA

THE BATH WAS refreshing although, unlike Carter, I washed my clothes first so they were mostly dry when I was finished. He stood glued to the fire for an hour in only his boxers. When I first came back from getting water while Marcus got ready for his bath, I had to stifle my laughter. Carter was standing as close to the fire as he could get without burning himself shivering. His teeth were chattering. I wanted to lie on the ground and laugh so hard I cried.

The sight of him standing in tennis shoes and his navy blue and white polka dot boxers was hilarious. It was by far the funniest thing that'd happened so far. I controlled myself though, and kept my attention on the water boiling.

Later that evening Marcus was bored so he went exploring. He came back sometime later with a rabbit and a squirrel. "These are some good woods we got here, man!" He said smiling. "Because of the stream, there are a lot of animals roaming around here."

"That's good to know," I said. "We can hunt before we leave tomorrow."

"We're leaving tomorrow?" Carter asked me almost in a whine.

"Of course. We have to get to Indianapolis." I said, dumbfounded. I didn't know why he thought we wouldn't be leaving.

Carter slumped back against a fallen down log and almost moped. I didn't know what had gotten into him lately, but he'd better get over it. I was in charge now and nothing was going to stop me from getting to Logan.

CHAPTER 42

LOGAN

I BUSTED OUT LAUGHING. I had to grab my stomach and tell myself to take deep breaths and to calm down. When I looked over at Maddie, I saw tears forming in her eyes. "Maddie! What's wrong?"

"What's wrong with you!" She shouted at me. "I just told you my deepest secret and you started guffawing!"

"Wait, you were serious about the whole you being a scientist thing?"

"Of course I was! Why would I make something like that up?" A tear slid out of her left eye and rolled down her cheek. I moved my thumb and wiped away the tear.

"I'm so sorry, Maddie. I shouldn't have laughed. That was an awful thing for me to do." She nodded her head and took a few deep breaths to keep from crying. I felt terrible. That was the worst possible thing I could have done. I didn't know what she thought of me now, but I knew I had to believe everything she said. I had to respect her feelings more. This was a very traumatic situation and obviously I was not making it any better.

I thought over what she told me. "So, you were a scientist? Wait. How old are you?"

"I'm only sixteen."

"Then how is that possible?"

"Well, when I was eight my mom lost her job. My dad has been gone since I was like six months old. My mom searched all over and couldn't find one anywhere. We had to move to Chicago because there was a better chance she could find a job. And she did... with the scientists.

My mom didn't want me staying by myself in a house in downtown Chicago, so she brought me to work with her. We practically lived with the scientists. I was homeschooled by a few of the scientists and I thought everything was great. I would help with data and casting experiments. I was in on all the inside jokes and life was great."

She paused and closed her eyes. "Then things went wrong. My mom never told me what happened, but two years ago my mom quit her job there, at least she said she quit. We moved to this small town called Michigan City. I missed all my friends at the science lab, but when I mentioned it my mom went ballistic. She told me never to say that again and she left it at that. A few months later my mom died of a heart attack in the middle of the night. The doctors said it was from trauma. They asked me if I knew what trauma she had been though."

Tears were constantly leaking and her voice was high and squeaky. I moved next to her and wrapped my arm around her shoulder, trying to comfort her but really it was just awkward so I pulled my arm back and just listened.

"How was I supposed to know? The only thing I remember from that night is that I was upset my mom had turned on my nightlight. I was too lazy to open my eyes and get out of bed to turn it off though. Of course, now I realize it wasn't my nightlight, but it was the scientists, but at the time I had no idea.

"Logan, I know they are behind this, but I don't know why. All I know is that we could be in serious danger."

CHAPTER 43

CARTER

ANA WAS TRUE to her word and in the morning she was itching to leave. "Can't we hunt before we go?" I asked.

She contemplated this and finally nodded her head. "Although I want to get going, it would probably be best to hunt. We just ate last night so anything we catch we will save for lunch or dinner later today."

We split up and traveled in three different directions. I wasn't sitting for half an hour when a rabbit hopped directly in front of my path. It was an easy target and I headed back to camp to wait for the others. I suspected they will both have kills so it was pointless for me to try for another.

Sure enough, Ana came back with a quail and Marcus had two squirrels.

"We are eating good tonight!" Marcus beamed.

"I think these animals are just stupid," I said. "We have gotten six all together. Obviously not many people pass through here."

"That's true," Ana said, "and you would think that because of the stream it would be a popular spot to stop and rest."

"Ana, you would need people for a spot to be popular," Marcus joked. "How many people have you seen around here? Not many I would suspect. They've all gone to their capitals for safety."

Ana surprised me and laughed. Maybe she was lightening up a little bit. She'd been on edge lately. I knew she was just anxious to help her brother, but it bothered me that Marcus made her laugh when it seemed I had only been irritating her lately. The three of us stomped through the woods not caring if anyone hears us and find the road. With water bottles filled, our stomachs full, and our bodies clean, we were all in high spirits.

Around three we decided to stop and eat something. I was not feeling well again. My arm was burning, but that was probably just because I didn't have anything to properly clean it with. I also felt faint and I was feeling exceptionally nauseous. But that had to be from walking all day. If I relaxed and ate something I hoped it would all go away and I'd feel fine. We decided to eat my rabbit for lunch and it tasted wonderful.

We set off again and my hopes were crushed. An hour later my head started pounding and my stomach ached again. I kept my mouth shut because there was no point in complaining. There was nothing we could do about it, plus I didn't want to irritate Ana any more than I already had. She was in a surprisingly cheerful mood and I wanted to keep it that way.

There was a bend in the road and when we were upon it, Ana stopped walking. "Look! It's a caravan!"

I lifted my head up to see it, but I didn't get a chance to. I felt awfully dizzy and all of a sudden I was falling into a deep, never-ending darkness.

CHAPTER 44

ANA

I TURNED AROUND TO share my findings with Carter and Marcus, but I saw Carter crash to the ground. "Carter!" I screamed. I dropped my pack to the ground and kneeled next to him on the ground. I rubbed my thumb over his cheek but he didn't respond. I rested my head upon his chest to check for a heartbeat. There was one, thank goodness.

I turned back and see Marcus pick up my backpack and I noticed the caravan traveling on west. "Marcus help me!" I shouted. He jogged over and handed me my backpack which I didn't see so he led my arms through it and placed on my back. I tried to lift up Carter by his armpits, but I couldn't stand. He was too heavy and I was too weak. I couldn't exactly say I'd been working out for the last few months. I'd been a little preoccupied.

"Here, let me take him." Marcus started to lift him up, but stopped. He gently laid Carter on the ground and shrugged off his backpack. Then he picked up Carter like a groom carried his bride. He took a deep breath and started walking slowly so I grabbed his backpack and followed behind him.

His breathing was heavy and it was clear he couldn't carry on for much longer. The caravan was getting too far away. We would never reach it in time. *What are we going to do?* I thought fast and made a decision. The backpacks were too much. As much as I hated to do it, I grabbed one of Carter's knives and I threw the backpacks to the side of the road. I took a deep breath and closed my eyes.

My feet started moving faster and faster until I was flying. The wind was blowing my hair back until it had all fallen out of the braid. My arms pumped back and forth for momentum. Saliva foamed at my mouth making it sticky and in need of a drink of water. My lips were dry and cracked. My throat burned with each gasp of air and my sides were cramping like no pain I've ever felt before. But I pushed all of that out of my head, choosing to focus on my destination. I focused on my running and I felt my feet smack the road with each step and I knew it was too much for my sneakers. It didn't matter. It was all happening in slow motion. As I grew nearer to the caravan I started yelling with all my might.

"Help me! Someone help me!" I screamed all the way. In what seemed like forever and in an instant at the same time I reached the last group of people that were hauling a trailer. "Help me!" I gasped. There was an old woman who turned around. She saw me and ordered the others in their group to stop. They instantly obeyed. "Do you have a doctor?" I asked, panting and drawing in breathes that raked through my lungs.

"Are you sick?" she asked me

"My friend! He's back there! I had to run and catch up with you. I don't know what happened, but he's in trouble."

She thought then pulled out a VCR. She turned it on and told someone on the other end to stop traveling. I could see the whole caravan stop and I couldn't help it but I started crying. I quickly wiped away the tears and turned around to see Marcus struggling with the two backpacks and Carter. It was too much for him and he stumbled to his knees.

"Can someone help him?" I shouted and I ran over to him. I pulled the two backpacks off of him and I called again for someone to help. I saw the old lady VCR someone and almost instantly I saw a man jogging from the caravan and kneeling down next to us. He scooped up Carter in his arms and he walked back into the crowd of the caravan.

He maneuvered through the throng of people and he stopped at one of the wagons. He opened the door and nestled inside was a cot. He laid Carter down and walked over to a shelf full of medical supplies. Marcus and I climbed in and closed the door behind us. I felt the wagon start to move so I positioned myself next Carter, brushing his hair out of his face while I wait.

I presumed the man was a doctor and he set a cold washcloth on Carter's forehead. "He's out cold. What happened to this boy?" He asked.

"I don't know," I said. "We were walking and he just fainted."

"Is he sick?"

I thought about this. Carter had been hot, but I hadn't noticed anything explicitly wrong with him. "I don't think so."

"Has he had any recent accidents?"

Then my stomach dropped. "He was attacked by a bear... but it was a few days ago! He never said anything about being sick or feeling unwell."

"What happened?"

"When he was attacked by a bear?" He nodded so I told him how the bear ran at him and tore up his arm. The doctor started pulling off Carter's shirt. "What are you doing?" I asked.

"I have to check out this wound. It could be infected."

Once the shirt was all the way off I was appalled by what I saw, and I had to swallow down the bile which was forming in my throat. Carter's injured arm was twice the size of his other arm. The wound had red streaking from it all the way down to his forearm. The claw marks never healed and were still open. The bandages we had first wrapped were gone. I had to look away before I puked.

"This doesn't look good," the doctor said. He first filled a syringe with a clear liquid and plunged it into his arm. He then pulled out a needle and thread to try and sew the wound back together. I couldn't look at the doctor I had to instead focus on Carter's face in case he woke up. After a good ten minutes the doctor said, "I don't think we will have to amputate it, but we will have to wait and see. I am going to leave you three alone and step out of the cart. I'll be right outside so come and find me when he wakes up. Until then continue putting cold water on his forehead. Change the washcloth every five minutes or so." He opened the door and hopped off the cart.

I took the liberty to change Carter's washcloth, and again tears formed. I tried to hold them back, but I couldn't. Tears fell. I felt a thumb wipe them away and I looked up to see Marcus standing next to me. His thumb lingered on my face just a second too long and I stood up. I wrapped my arms around his neck and his arms wrapped around my waist. I cried on his shoulder until I realized how weak I looked and took a deep breath. I was being ridiculous. I fumbled with the excuse of having to put more cold water on Carter's wash cloth and pulled away.

I wiped my hand across my eyes to completely stop the tears and took a deep breath. This was ridiculous. I should not have cried in front of Marcus. I should not have shown any weakness. I had to be strong for Carter and I couldn't if I was crying. I refilled his washcloth and laid it across his forehead and I rubbed his cheek with my thumb.

But then Carter started to stir.

CHAPTER 45

LOGAN

"WHAT DO YOU think we should do?" I asked Maddie.

"I don't know. We have to get out of here, but we can't yet."

"Why not?" I asked her.

"Well, I don't know about you, but obviously I'm not strong enough yet. We need to start working out. Like therapy! I don't even think I've moved from this spot since we got here. I have to say my butt is sore!"

I cracked up laughing.

"I'm serious!" Maddie said. She tried to stand up and I could tell she was in agony. She managed to stand up though. I followed suit and realized my leg didn't hurt as much as I thought it would. I took a step though and pain shot through my leg. I wanted to scream out, but I bit my lip and took another step. Maddie did the same, but after two steps she had to sit back down.

I managed to walk ten paces before I decided I needed to rest. I sat down next to Maddie who was stretching. She leaned over and wrapped her hands around her feet. She did other leg stretches to help strengthen her legs.

"We need to do this every day a few times a day," Maddie said. "Then we need to start running... although if we work out too much they might think we are planning to escape."

"Or we could just be working out so we don't get fat."

"Yeah, on this five-course meal? I'm sure that's what they will think." Maddie said sarcastically then laughed and it sounded happy and light. It was the kind of laugh that made me want to laugh along with her and so I did. I looked into her bright, blue eyes. They were twinkling and she looked back at me. For a moment we just stared at each other and I felt a connection between us. She broke the bond and continued stretching.

I reached for my toes, but I couldn't concentrate on stretching. I was thinking about those happy, blue eyes and I knew that I wanted to make sure those eyes were always happy.

CHAPTER 46

CARTER

I OPENED MY EYES and I wanted to scream. I contained myself though and just let out a short, hoarse noise. Spiders. There were spiders all over me. At first I froze and watched them in disbelief. Most were frozen but when I screamed they started to move. I could see hundreds of small sets of eight legs all over my body. They were crawling up my legs, creeping closer to me.

More spiders leaped onto me from the bookshelves and the ground. They were everywhere. There were brown spiders, and black hairy spiders. Some with huge eyes boring into me, threatening me, and others were tiny-bodied but quick. No matter what shape they were they were all menacing. Their tiny, beady eyes were watching me as if they had found their target and were closing in on it. I waved my arms and shouted to scare them away, but they just marched closer to me. I tried to brush them away with my hands but when I knocked a few away the others quickly closed the gap again.

I started panicking, my breaths coming short and fast and I was almost to the point of tears I was so afraid.

Right before they finally reached me I saw Ana. *Is it Ana?* I tried to warn her to get away from the spiders before they saw her too. It was too late though and the spiders were upon me.

CHAPTER 47

ANA

I WOKE UP BECAUSE I heard Carter scream. I stood up and looked into his eyes which were focusing on something far away. They were wide with fear and he was sweating profusely. He started beating at the sheets and shouting. I looked at him with a look of confusion because nothing was there. He was just batting at the blanket I placed over him.

All of a sudden he stopped swatting at the sheet and began to cry. I yelled for the doctor and he came rushing in. When he saw Carter crying he asked what in the world was going on. I told the doctor how Carter screamed and was freaking out with the blanket and the doctor quickly ran to his medical shelf.

"He's hallucinating."

"Why?"

"From the medicine. Hold on…" He rummaged around in the cabinets until he pulled out a needle. He stuck it in Carter's arm and Carter fell asleep instantly. "I gave him some medicine to help with the pain in his arm and it must have caused him to hallucinate. I'll have to find some other medicine for him." Once the doctor was satisfied with his findings he loaded another shot and gave it to Carter in his other arm.

"What's strange," the doctor said, "is that the medicine shouldn't have caused him to hallucinate. I've used this concoction many times and not once have I seen a hallucination occur from it. We'll try this other medicine for a while and see what happens."

"He might have had a reaction to the medication, though," I said. "How many other patients have you used it with?"

"Oh, I would say about eight or nine hundred."

My mouth dropped open and I quickly closed it. "That many!" I squeaked.

"Well, I was only a doctor for a few months before World War III. I didn't get a chance to use it too many times especially since I'm not a surgeon." The doctor paused and shifted his gaze from me to Carter. "We will see what happens with this medicine, but I don't think the pain killer had anything to do with the hallucination."

"What do you think is causing it, then?" I asked. I was almost afraid to hear the answer.

"That bear. Whatever diseases it carried around with it might have been given to Carter when it attacked him."

"But he was only scratched by the bear, how can that be possible?"

"Have you looked at his wound?" the doctor asked me.

I shook my head no.

"It's hard to tell because there are so many scratches, but when I was dressing the wound I noticed a few holes. Most of them you can't see because of the scratches, but that bear bit Carter in the arm before he scratched Carter."

"What? Carter never told me this."

"I don't know if he knew himself. Many times the brain blocks out horrible memories such as this and he might only remember being scratched because the effects are clearly visible. From what I can tell from this wound, Carter has been suffering for a while now." The doctor took off the bandages and was inspecting Carter's arm. I didn't have the guts to look at it.

"He never told me he was in pain,"

"What's the point, you couldn't have done anything and the boy knew that."

"He still should have told me!"

"We cannot change the decisions made in the past. We have to live with the consequences and figure out how to deal with them. I don't know what's going on in his body. I don't have the medical instruments

I need to find out anyways. But from the condition he's in you can thank your lucky stars you found us when you did."

I stared solemnly at Carter while he slept, the regret in the pit of my stomach gnawing away at me almost unbearably.

"All we can do is watch what he does and work on his reactions to diagnose something and figure out how to cure it."

"Alright." And with that, the doctor stepped out of the enclosed cart.

CHAPTER 48

ANA

THE NEXT WEEK passed by slowly. Carter slept through most of it, but when he was not sleeping he was hallucinating. I'd heard him talk about butterflies, snow, and one time he even said Marcus.

Marcus spent most of the time outside the cart walking around and meeting new people. He was only inside to sleep. I stayed with Carter throughout the week, but after four days of being enclosed to the small space I couldn't take another minute of it.

I opened the door of the cart and jumped out while it was still moving. Since most people were walking the carts and vans were moving slowly like an old-fashioned parade. My grandmas used to tell me about parades that walked through the streets instead of flying and weaving through the crowds. I felt like I was in a blast to the past – all the way back to 2045.

I walked behind the medicine cart for a few minutes before I decided to search for Marcus. I weaved my way through the crowd. I had never realized how big this caravan was until now. We were walking up a hill and when we reached the top I looked down at the caravan before me and I watched the people and vans and carts walking before me as far as I could see. Although there was a wood about half a mile in front of me that we were passing through which obstructed my line of vision, I was still amazed.

I wondered where all these people were going. They were headed in the direction of Indianapolis, but they probably should have been traveling to Washington D.C. where York said a new foundation for our country was being built.

York.

I hadn't thought of York in weeks. I wondered where we went. He said he was coming after Carter and me, but we hadn't seen any sign of him. He must have found other people to take to Washington D.C.

I thought about this subject for too long and tried to focus my thoughts on my surroundings. I realized I'd stopped walking and I didn't want anyone to run into me so I took a step down the hill in search of Marcus once again. It didn't take me long before I spotted him talking to a man.

I ran up to them and said a quick "hello".

Marcus stopped his conversation with the man to introduce me. "Tom Gable, this is Ana…"

"Talley. I'm Ana Talley."

Marcus looked at me. "See, that's something I didn't know about you. I was telling Tom, here, about Carter. What's his last name?"

I thought. I knew Carter had told me before. I thought back to when we first met in the forest behind my house and I smiled. I was so rude to him. "Jones," I said.

"Right, Carter Jones. I was telling Tom about what happened to him and my adventure on how the three of us ended up here."

"Yeah, well, that's just great," I said. I continued on sarcastically. "So, Tom, sorry to end your interesting conversation here with Marcus."

Tom just smiled at me then chuckled. He turned to Marcus and whispered something in his ear. Marcus grinned then took my arm. "Alright, Tom. I'll find you later and we can finish our conversation."

Tom nodded a farewell and Marcus led me to the center of the caravan.

"What did he say to you?" I asked Marcus.

He laughed, "Oh, nothing."

"I'm serious, tell me!"

"Fine, he said you're feisty."

"What?"

"Never mind. You would have had to hear the rest of our conversation, which I must say you so rudely interrupted."

"It doesn't matter that much does it? You can always talk to him later."

"Yeah, I guess but that's not the point. The world doesn't revolve around you, Ana."

I glared at Marcus. "Never mind, Marcus. I'm just wasting my time anyways." I turned and stormed away. He called after me but I ignored him and made my way back to Carter instead.

CHAPTER 49

CARTER

I OPENED MY EYES and saw Ana asleep in a chair at the end of my bed. I accidentally sneezed and Ana's head snapped up. "I'm sorry," I whispered. "Go back to sleep."

Ana wiped her tired eyes. "It's okay. How are you feeling?" She asked sleepily.

"Better than I did yesterday. When we were hiking I thought I was going to pass out."

"Carter, we've been with this caravan for almost a whole week."

"A whole week! And wait, a caravan? Where are we?"

Ana filled me in on how I passed out right when we found this caravan and that she'd been riding along with me all week, waiting for me to finally come to my senses and wake up. "I don't know where we are though. I should go ask," she said. "I'll bring the doctor in too."

She opened the door and jumped to the ground. I watched her disappear as she closed the door and she waved before she was gone.

I took the time to look around the room. It was pretty plain except for a narrow walk way around my bed, two chairs I assumed were for Ana and Marcus, a shelf full of medicine, and... *what is that?* In the corner of the room, crouching, trying to stay out of sight was a panther. I thought they were only found in... not Indiana! It growled and I kept myself from shouting. I closed my eyes and leaned back on my pillow.

I tried to stay calm when I heard the door creak. My eyes flew open and I saw Ana entering my room. "Be careful!" I whispered to her just loudly enough so she could hear without scaring the panther. The smile left her face and she became solemn.

"What, Carter?" She asked me.

"Shh! Keep your voice down!" I whispered harshly. I pointed to the corner and when she looked, A bemused expression crossed her face. She looked to me for an explanation but I was growing more nervous by the second. "The panther! Leave, quickly!" Ana looked shocked and she jumped out of the room and called for the doctor. She left the door open though and the panther stalked to the opening and leapt out. "Ana!" I yelled. She came rushing back to me. "The panther escaped! It's out there somewhere!"

She came in the room and sat on the chair next to me, taking my hand. "Shh, Carter. Everything is alright. Everything is alright." She said the words to me, but it looked as if she were reassuring herself instead.

CHAPTER 50

LOGAN

As the first week of "therapy" came to an end I was exhausted. Maddie and I had been working out for hours at a time. Although it's not what I used to call working out, it's having the same effect. Before the beast came along, running a few miles would have been a good workout for my legs, but now, since my leg was torn up, just walking a mile hurt. The cut in my leg went through all my muscle so it instantly became weak.

The beast did the same to Maddie's leg. I couldn't say which one of us was healing faster. I'd like to say myself because I was able to rest longer before we started, but now that I thought about it, resting might have caused the muscles to weaken even more, whereas Maddie could almost instantly start working her muscles so they didn't become as frail.

Maybe we were at about the same spot. All I knew was that we weren't getting out of here any time soon.

The beast began bringing us food regularly and water sporadically. I wanted to figure out where the beast slept, ate, lived. He was so strange. I hadn't told Maddie this yet, but once my leg was better, before we escaped, I was going to figure out where it lived and how it lived. I could be on the verge of a scientific discovery. If only our parents knew about this. They would have been fascinated.

Wait. I thought back to when Maddie was telling me about her life before all this happened. She said the scientists were behind this – maybe. My parents were scientists. They couldn't be... No. I pushed the thoughts out of my mind. There was no way they would ever do something like this. I needed to stay focus on exercising, escaping, and figuring out the beast.

CHAPTER 51

ANA

"THERE'S SOMETHING SERIOUSLY wrong, Doctor Fern!" I exclaimed. The doctor came rushing in and put Carter asleep again to get rid of his hallucinations. "This is the fourth or fifth time this week Carter's woken up and hallucinated and did not remember the previous incidents!"

Doctor Fern sighed. "I know there is something wrong, but until I can find the source of what's causing them, there's nothing I can do about it. I don't want to keep putting him to sleep like this. I might need this medication for other patients, and it can't be good for his health. He's going to go on a sleeping overload."

"Then what should we do?" I asked.

"I don't know if there is anything we can do at this point. I've been trying to pin point this germ for days but I can't find anything wrong! It's so frustrating! I have a small microscope, but I couldn't bring all of my machines with me. There's just not enough room. I've looked at his blood, his cells, his tissue, and I can't find anything out of order. The thing is I know something's wrong."

"Obviously something is wrong! He's hallucinating about panthers and butterflies!" I didn't feel like it was a good idea to mention that he had hallucinated about Marcus and myself though.

"I'm going to take another look at his blood. I'll need my space though, so if you would please leave and come back in a few hours I'd appreciate it."

"I'm not leaving Carter."

"I wasn't giving you a choice, young lady."

Doctor Fern glared at me and pointed to the door in that serious way doctors do when they need to concentrate. I hopped out of the moving cart and slammed the door. I started to walk away, but I stopped. I forgot to tell Carter how close we were getting to Indianapolis. In just a few days we would be there and we could begin our search for Logan. I thought about Doctor Fern though, and decided it would be better to wait to tell Carter. He wasn't even awake anyhow.

I walked through the caravan and stopped to talk to an old lady I saw. She told me that her name was Beth Maine. I decided to talk to her because she looked interesting to me. I thought it might be nice to talk to someone who grew up a long time ago, in the 2040's, before all this war stuff happened.

She told me a little about her life, but what was really interesting was that she used to be a potter, a profession I thought had died out decades ago. She had a small cart I didn't notice before, but her brother was steering it. Inside the cart were at least twenty different pots she had made. There were blue, green, and the standard clay color, all with white intricate designs. One I especially admired was a small teal colored pot with flowers all over it. The opening of the pot was rounded and curved giving off the impression that it was a flower.

"Why do you like pottery so much?" I asked her. "Nobody uses it today."

She smiled. "I know, and maybe that's the reason I like it so much. I like the mystery of it, it intrigues me. I'm trying to keep a little bit of my mother's hobby and my childhood with me through these whirlwind times. You know, the ancient Greeks and Romans used to use pottery all the time. Sometimes they would paint stories onto the pots."

"Did you paint a story on any of your pots?"

"Sadly, no. I was in the middle of making a pot when the war struck. I thought about painting on a story. But I realized I didn't need to. The pot in itself is a story enough," she said rotating a small clay masterpiece around in her hands. She suddenly turned to me. "Do you read the Bible?"

"No. I don't think I really believe in that stuff."

She nodded. "We all believe what we believe. Well, in the Bible there is a verse from Isaiah. It says that the Lord is the potter and we are his clay and we are all the work of His hand. Well, my pots are the work of my hands." She stopped talking and stared at the little cart holding her pottery with a soft smile on her face as if she had explained everything. Confused I asked her to explain.

Instead she asked me, "Have you ever made a pot before?" I shook my head no and she continued. "I'll have to teach you sometime. Maybe one night when we stop to sleep. Before the sun disappears and there is still light."

"I'd like that," I said.

The next evening, once the caravan had stopped for the night, I wove my way through the campsites until I found Beth. When she saw me approached she smiled and said, "I was so hoping you would come back."

Beth pulled out a small wooden turning table and stool and then plopped a slab of clay on top. She set a bucket of water next to me and told me to start pressing the clay. I dipped my hands in the water and squeezed the clay and I could feel it squish between my fingers. It was cold and stuck to my hands creating a layer of clay on them. Being dirty was a feeling I had gotten used to, but this was different. It was actually refreshing.

I pushed the clay into the table, folding it over and over as Beth instructed until my arms were sore and I was contemplating why I needed to do this. "You are getting all of the air pockets out," Beth told me as if she had read my mind. "Air pockets will create bubbles in the clay and can cause the pot to explode in the kiln.

"Now," she said, "you want to plop your clay down in the middle of your turn table here." And I did as she instructed. "Start pressing your foot on the pedal, slowly at first that way the clay doesn't just fly off!" She waited for me to move the table at a moderate yet constant pace before she began instructing me again. "You want to cup your hands around the clay, surrounding it and protecting it, molding it to the round shape you desire. And then one you start to get a smooth shape you want to stick both your thumbs into the clay, pushing almost entirely to the bottom but not quite all the way."

She waited patiently as I tried and failed to make my pot. The first time the pot was hopelessly lopsided, the second time I pressed my thumbs all the way to the bottom and the third time I squeezed my palms together too tightly created a long skinny vase instead. Right when I was about to give up though I managed to shape it accordingly. I threw my hands up in victory but I accidentally pressed down on the foot pedal and the wheel spun out of control, throwing my pot off the table and smashing it on the ground.

My mouth flew open, my hands falling hopelessly to my sides. "I will never get this right!" I exclaimed.

Beth picked up my clay and slopped it back on the wheel. "Give it one more try, Ana." And so with an exasperated sigh I did. To my amazement I started the wheel, kept my hands steady when they were pressed against the shaping clay and slowly pressed my thumbs into the clay, cautiously stopping them at the perfect spot. I pulled them to the outsides to open the hole so I could create a bowl shape and then slowed the wheel, making sure to come to a complete stop before I got excited.

I peeled my pot off of the wheel, holding it in my hands and knowing I had molded it to perfection. And that's when I figured out what Beth had been talking about. That verse was about how God molded each of us in his eyes to perfection. And maybe I wasn't entirely sure what to think about religion at that moment, but one thing I felt was hope. A beautiful, perfect hope.

CHAPTER 52

ANA

I LEFT BETH AND traveled on down the road until I stumbled across Marcus. He was at the very front of the caravan. The sun was starting to set and I felt a cool May breeze on my face. One by one the caravan stopped. I walked the few paces left until I had closed the distance and was standing next to Marcus. We had reached the end of a forest and stretching out before me for miles in every direction was a canyon.

Marcus and I stared in awe. I noticed Tom Gable was standing on the other side of Marcus.

"What is this?" I said in disbelief.

"How did this happen?" Marcus asked Tom.

He shrugged his shoulders. "Although I think we cross off erosion on our list of possible answers."

Marcus laughed. It helped lighten the mood, but the same question was pounding itself in my brain and I was sure everyone else's brain. I dared to say it. "How are we going to cross that?"

Silence.

Then Tom spoke. "We will find a way. We've traveled through worse."

"Worse than this? A ten mile wide canyon?" My jaw almost hung open.

"Yeah, you're right, we really haven't." Tom smiled and Marcus and I laughed.

Then I remembered Carter. "I have to go tell Carter!"

"Good. Spread the word. We are going to camp here the rest of the night," Tom informed us. Marcus followed me as I turned and jogged towards Carter.

As I was running through the crowd, no one seemed to believe me when I said we were stopping because a canyon was blocking our way. *That didn't seem too outrageous did it?* Don't answer that. People just ignored me, stared at me like I was a lunatic, and the worst – laughed. I tried to ignore the people who laughed at me and focused on spreading the news.

I started telling people that Tom told me to notify everyone though and they started to listen more. He must have been pretty important. I saw Beth and stopped to tell her the news. I was panting from running, but once my breath came back I told her the whole story.

Unlike everyone else, Beth believed me. "It's the biggest canyon I've seen in my whole life," I told her.

"Have you been to the Grand Canyon?" She asked me.

"No, but I'm sure this is bigger."

"I don't want to disappoint you, dear, but it's probably not." She chuckled and patted me on the back.

"I'd love to stay longer, but I have to go tell Carter."

"I'm going to see Tom anyways. Bye dear."

Marcus and I set off again and in a few minutes we reached Carter. Doctor Fern was just stepping out of the room and looked confused. "Ana, what is going on?"

"We are stopping here for the night,"

"But it's still light out," Doctor Fern looked up at the sky and towards the setting sun.

Marcus took over the conversation, "There is a small dilemma on the road ahead. Tom is instructing everyone to stay put because we are staying here for the night. If you have any more questions I advise you to ask Tom because he's the only one who has any clue what's going on."

"Tom told you to stay put?"

Marcus nodded. "That is correct."

"Alright then, I'll go talk to him. You can see Carter, but he might be out of it for a while. Just hang tight. I'm this close to figuring out what is going on." She held her fingers close together then walked off.

Marcus and I stepped into Carter's room and we saw him asleep on the bed. Marcus sat against the wall silently as I crossed the room and sat on the edge of Carter's bed. He is so peaceful when he is sleeping. All of a sudden a wave or fatigue hit me. I hadn't slept well recently because I'd been so worried about Carter, so I rested my head on his pillow and curled up beside Carter and fell asleep.

I woke suddenly. It was a nightmare. I was dreaming that York was back and he was hunting us down. I shook the dream out of my head and I opened my eyes fully and saw Carter watching me. I sat upright and looked around. Marcus was sleeping in the corner and Carter was just lying next to me, silent.

"How long have I been asleep?" I asked Carter.

"I don't know I've only been up for about ten minutes."

I stood up and I walked over to the door. I peeked outside and seeing that the orange and pink streaks of dawn were starting to appear in the sky, I turned back and sat across from Carter. "It's early in the morning. Do you want some breakfast?"

"I'm alright for right now. Maybe I'll have lunch in a few hours."

I protested. "You need to eat Carter. You need to regain your strength."

"I'll regain it at lunch."

"Why won't you listen to me?"

Carter shrugged. "I'm just not hungry right now."

I would have argued longer with Carter except Doctor Fern walked in. "You're up," she said, "good. I need to talk with the both of you."

CHAPTER 53

CARTER

DOCTOR FERN SET down her clipboard on the counter and she took a deep breath before she began talking. "I've run tests and tests and I've figured it out. There is a disease in your body that is attaching itself to you. To your cells. It was destroying them and making them weak, and destroying your immune system and just about everything else. But… now it's receding. The bacteria have stopped multiplying and they are dying off. I looked through the samples I've taken over the last few weeks and at first the "population" was growing and growing, but now its numbers are diminishing.

"Don't ask me why or how, but somehow your body has fought off the disease. I'm just winging it here, but I would say that in a few days you should be fine again. This bacterium is peculiar though. It might have long term effects that I have do not know about or it might just be in remission. Still, don't get all crazy and try to run a marathon anytime soon, okay? Take it easy."

With that she poured me a glass of water and walked out. Ana was all smiles. She leaned down and gave me a hug. Marcus gave me a knuckle-touch and said "way to go, bro." Knowing the disease was going away put me in high spirits, but it didn't give me any more energy. I was exhausted and soon fell asleep.

I dreamt a nightmare. The scene of when the bear attacked me replayed in my head over and over each time with a different ending. The first time was how it happened. But the second time, the bear didn't die from my bullets and it nearly killed me. I shook awake – or so I thought, but when I opened my eyes I was in the same spot in the woods and the bear was coming at me. Then a second bear just as gruesome as the first jumped out of the woods and came after me. The twist in the last dream was the worst. Ana came to help me, but I hadn't killed the bear and it attacked her. This dream sent me bolting upright screaming her name.

I felt arms wrapped around me and someone rubbing my back whispering incomprehensible words. When my mind clears itself I fully open my eyes to Ana holding me. She pushed herself back to arm's length and stared at me. "What's wrong Carter?"

"It was horrible. A nightmare. But that's all it was – just a dream. I'm sorry if I woke you up. How long have we been traveling today?"

She shook her head. "You were only sleeping a few hours. Three at most. And I didn't get a chance to tell you. We have been stopped for hours. We aren't moving because there is an enormous canyon blocking our way. It's ten miles wide in every direction, Carter. It's amazing. I made a trip to see it as the son was rising and it casted a warm glow across the entire vastness of the canyon. It was… indescribable."

"It sounds incredible," I pondered the idea and tried to imagine what the canyon looked like in my mind. "How are we going to cross it, though?"

"I have no idea. My guess is very slowly." She laughed and pulls her hair back into a pony tail.

"You're not in charge anymore," I smirked. "How does it feel?"

She stuck her nose in the air, showing the Ana I met in the woods that first day. "If I were in charge we would be halfway through that canyon already," she retorted.

"Really? Have you ever been to the Grand Canyon?"

"No, but it doesn't matter. It can't be all that difficult to cross. You just need a little time, right?"

CHAPTER 54

ANA

WRONG. WE HAD been sitting here for two days waiting for Tom to explain how we were going to travel through this canyon. Finally, Tom said we would start moving… one vehicle at a timee. And Carter's was at the back. There were only about twenty vehicles behind us.

By the time we started moving Carter was feeling better. The morning our vehicle reached the canyon, Carter stood up and walked. He walked alongside the vehicle for a few minutes, but once we reached the actual canyon, he had to rest again. The disease wasn't totally gone and he was still weak. He was able to look out at the vast openness of the canyon thought and it took his breath away. He stared out at it silently for a few minutes before climbing back inside the cart.

I was excited when we finally were able to start heading down the canyon. The caravan had formed some-what of a path in the rock, but Tom was directing us most of the way. It was harder that I thought it would be.

The canyon side was steep and treacherous. There were tiny stones and gravel all over the path, not to mention the boulders that threatened to rain down on us. We were the last group of the day to head down into the middle of the canyon where everyone else was waiting, and it was starting to get dark.

I tried not to think about the dangers, but I was afraid. I realized that I was afraid of heights, or more specifically, of falling from heights. Staring down into a canyon can definitely prompt you to fear heights. I was so nervous of stepping on a rock or tripping over my own feet that I often fell behind and had to hurry to catch up.

When we finally reached the bottom I was filled with joy. I stepped into Carter's room to rest. I was tired of being paranoid.

I woke in the morning to a scream and a gunshot. I ran outside and saw that another group was heading down towards us. There was a lady running around screaming about her ankle. I heard the words, "ankle, long, sting, and venom." It wasn't hard to connect the dots and realized she was bit by a snake. Being in the canyon though, there was no way to help her. Doctor Fern was nowhere in sight and even if she was she couldn't get up to where the lady was in time to save her.

When the group reached the bottom we attempted to bury the woman. We placed stones around her body because the ground was too hard to dig into. Everyone was solemnly standing around her, paying their respects quietly except a man who was crying whom I guessed to be her husband. Even with the tragic mood of the morning we had to continue on. By the end of the day everyone was down in the depths of the canyon. We camped out one more night and in the morning we were able to start moving.

Right in the center of the canyon was a small stream. There were a few shrubs, but for this part of the trip we would be relying on whatever canned goods people had stored and brought along with them.

We certainly enjoyed the stream though. Marcus and I convinced Carter to come with us and the three of us ran into the stream and relaxed in the cool water. It was refreshing in the eighty degree heat. Some other travelers joined us and we met a few teens. Molly and Matt were a couple who were both eighteen and had been dating for a few years.

Molly was gorgeous. She was a little taller than me, but still short. She had beautiful blond, naturally curly hair that reached her shoulders, and the sun sparkled in her big, brown eyes. Matt was equally handsome. He was some-what tall, maybe five-ten, with dark brown hair and matching dark brown eyes. Molly and Matt were cute together. Matt had a great idea to play chicken. Carter wasn't up to it and sat on the bank and watched instead.

Marcus and I had been talking strategy when Matt yelled, "Quit talking and let's play! You're going down Marcus!"

Marcus bent down and I sat on his shoulders. He stood up and we faced Molly and Matt.

"Are you ready, Ana?" Molly yelled.

"Oh yeah!" A crowd formed at the edge of the water and I saw Carter talking to a girl who sat down next to him to watch us. I was distracted by them and when Molly's hands grabbed my upper arms I was surprised and nearly fell off Marcus.

I reached and held onto Molly's arms. Instead of managing to push each other off, it was as if we were holding on to each other to stay on our boys' shoulders. I decided to try another tactic. I quickly let go of Molly's arm and poked her stomach. She screamed and let go of my arms to hide her stomach and while she was moving her arms to her stomach I pushed her shoulders. Marcus and I hollered as we watched Molly and Matt fall backwards into the water. Marcus raised his arms in the air. He opened his hands up towards me and I high-fived him.

"I want a rematch!" Matt yelled.

"What?" Marcus challenged. "You ready to face defeat a second time?"

"Oh it's on!" Molly hopped up on his shoulders again and the chicken war started all over again. By nightfall, Marcus and I came out victorious with eight wins to five. When I got out of the water though, I wanted to give Carter a hug and see what he thought of the chicken war, but he wasn't there.

When Marcus and I walked back to our vehicle, I expected Carter to be sleeping so I was quiet. But, when I opened the door and stepped in, Carter wasn't inside the room. "Have you seen Carter?" I asked Marcus.

"No, I haven't seen him since earlier today when we were playing chicken." He thought hard. "Well, I did see him with some girl. He might have gone off with her somewhere. Oh well."

Marcus grabbed a towel and stepped back outside. He said he preferred to sleep outside. I decided to change since no one was in the room, but I couldn't shake what Marcus had said. *Carter? Off with some girl?* And why did I feel a pang of jealousy and hurt come over me? We certainly were not together in any way. I tried to shake away the thoughts, and once I was in dry clothes I took advantage of the empty bed and went to sleep.

CHAPTER 55

LOGAN

THREE STRAIGHT WEEKS of exercising was enough. I could walk a few miles and run half a mile. I was fed up and restless just staying here waiting for something to happen.

"Maddie, we have to do something. I don't want to just stay here and I'm tired with just staying here waiting for something to happen. Maddie, we have to do something. I don't want to just stay here and exercise the rest of my life."

"Okay, what do you want to do?"

"I'm not sure, but something. The only way something is going to happen is if we make it happen. I have an idea. Let's figure out this beast. Let me ask you something." She stared at me. "Do you know where this beast lives?"

"Here," she stated.

"But where here! I mean, how big is this place? We've only seen a few yards of this place. Who knows how much of it there is. Second, how many beasts are there? How do we know it's the same beast that keeps bringing us food and water and not a few different beasts? And third, and maybe the best question, where does the beast get the food and water from? There has to be a stream and some kind of fruit source and everything else."

"You're right," she said.

"I know I'm right," I joked. "I'm serious though. Let's figure this thing out. I know what you told me, but what if we discover something besides everything the scientists know."

"That sounds like an adventure."

"Exactly! So, let's say… tomorrow. Tomorrow morning we will head out and try to figure out this beast."

"Sounds like a plan."

In the morning Maddie shook me awake. "Are you ready to go?"

"Yeah, let me wake up." I stood up and did a few jumping jacks. I loosened up my limbs and retied my tennis shoes. "Should we bring the bucket?"

Maddie shrugged. "Do you think we will need it?"

"Why not?" I picked up the water bucket which was almost empty and Maddie and I started to walk. We saw a lot of what we usually see: concrete, gravel, no signs of life, lingering smoke. After an hour of walking and no change in scenery, Maddie was ready to give up.

"Maybe there isn't anything out there. Maybe it's all concrete."

"There has to be something, Maddie! How has the beast been getting the food and water?"

"Maybe from the scientists or something, I don't know."

"We have to keep going though, not only to find the beast's home, but to find a way out of here. I have to go home to find my sister. I have to make sure she's okay. I have to protect her. And I can't do that from in here."

Maddie pulled me in a hug. I couldn't cry. Not because I am a boy and not because I'm trying to be brave. I just couldn't. We continued walking and all of a sudden Maddie tripped on a rock. She almost fell to the ground, but I caught her mid-fall. I gently lowered her to the ground and she rubbed her foot. "Where is it?" She asked to herself. She felt along the ground until she found what she tripped over. To both of our surprises, it wasn't a rock. It was a root. It looked like a tree root that was partially sticking out of the ground.

"What the heck?" I wondered aloud.

"I'm not sure. Let's keep walking and see if we find anything else along the way."

Not very long after, I stumbled on a root. "Another one! We have to be getting close to some kind of vegetation. These roots have to lead to something."

They led to something alright. A hundred yards later Maddie and I stopped walking. We gazed ahead of us and stared up at an enormous tree. It had to be a hundred feet tall and fifty feet wide. Its bark was dark brown and its branches were lush with bright green leaves and all kinds of fruit. There were apples growing all over it along with oranges, fruit shaped like stars, and other fruit I've never seen before. The weirdest fruit are the bananas which I thought were extinct. I've only seen them in old TV re-runs.

"Have you ever had a banana, Maddie?"

"No, but I've always wanted to try one. My great-grandmother said they were her favorite."

"Okay, let's try to get one down," I suggested.

"How are we supposed to reach them? They are at least fifty feet above our heads!"

"There has to be some way. The beast gets them down."

"Has it ever brought us a banana before? I don't think so," she smart-mouthed me.

"But it did bring us apples," I argued.

We spent the rest of the day trying to throw rocks into the tree and knock down a banana, but to no avail. We accidentally hit an apple that came flying down, but no bananas. "It's really quiet," I whispered to Maddie as we sat under the tree.

"Yeah, something's not right."

"Do you think it's odd that we haven't seen the beast all day?"

CHAPTER 56

CARTER

"I REALLY SHOULD GET back. My friends are going to be wondering where I am," I told Cindy. Cindy was seventeen with blonde hair and blue eyes. We were watching Ana and Marcus play chicken earlier today in the stream, but after four or five matches we grew bored and decided to go somewhere else.

I was trying to get away without hurting her feelings, but she kept talking. She was rather annoying. Finally, when it was pitch black outside, I was able to get away. I snuck through the caravan and tried not to look suspicious. All of a sudden, someone popped out from behind one vehicle. It startled me and I stopped in my tracks. "Sorry," I stammered and tried to walk around the man and continue on.

He side stepped me and stood directly in front of me. I was uncomfortable being so close and took a step back. "Do I know you?" I asked, looking up for the first time. The man looked familiar, but it was too dark to see his facial features.

"I know you." He stood there and stared at me. I could see the whites of his eyes in the dark of the night. They looked like a cat's eyes. "Well, I'm going to bed." The man smiled slightly and stepped out of my way.

Chills went down my spine. I speed walked until I didn't think the man could see me then I ran the rest of the way. When I opened the door and walked into my room there was nothing more I wanted than to lie down in my bed and forget what happened in a deep, peaceful sleep, but Ana was there. She was sprawled out over my bed sleeping soundly. I didn't have the heart to wake her.

Instead I grabbed a blanket and curled up on the floor next to her. It didn't take long before I was out.

There was pain on my stomach and I yelled awake. I heard a yelp and looked up and saw Ana. She had one hand on her heart and another covering her eyes. "Carter! What are you doing down there! I stepped on you and you scared everything out of me!"

I laughed and sat up on my elbows. "Did you have a good night's sleep?"

"I did, thank you very much," Ana retorted. "When did you get back? I thought you were with some girl." Her voice had a little snide in it.

"Ugh, don't remind me. That girl talked and talked. I had to pry myself away from her last night." When I said that something in Ana changed. It wasn't like she plastered a huge smile on her face or laughed, it was something subtle. A small change in her posture, in her eyes. "Did you have fun with Marcus yesterday? How was chicken?" I asked.

"It was great! We won eight to five. I really want to hang out with Molly and Matt again today. You should join us."

"Alright, sounds good."

We both stood up and headed outside. I decided not to tell Ana about the man from last night even though he kept popping into my mind and clawing at me. There was something about him I didn't like. Maybe what he said to me. 'I know you.' It was... not what I would have expected him to say. As if he were waiting for me to recognize him. And the voice... I shuddered and tried to forget about it. I didn't want Ana to know anything was wrong yet.

We spent the day with Marcus, Molly, and Matt just traveling and talking. Ana was right, they are really cool people. After a few hours I was tired and said goodbye. I needed to lie down and rest. I reached my room and opened the door. I jumped in quickly so I wouldn't fall while it was moving, and closed the door. I latched the door closed and turned around.

Standing before me was York.

"Hello, Carter," he said. "Remember me? I remember you."

My jaw dropped. York was the one who stopped me last night. That's why he had seemed familiar. I did know him.

"Cat got your tongue?"

I swear that was his favorite line. Just like his eerie cat eyes. "How did you find us?"

"I decided to join the caravan, look for people to take with me to Washington D.C. I saw your girlfriend playing in the stream with another man. How's your relationship going?"

"We are not – oh never mind." York didn't care and never would care about things like that.

"Then," he continued, "I saw you talking to another girl. I just followed you two a couple yards behind until you finally decided to leave. I stopped you on your way home last night. I wanted to see if you remembered me, that's all." A sly grin appeared on his face. No, that wasn't all.

"What do you want, York," I demanded.

He leaned against the wall. "Oh, nothing new. Just what I wanted before."

"Get out."

"Taking charge I see?" York smiled.

"Now. Leave us alone. We aren't going with you."

"Don't worry, I'm not going to force you. I want you two to decide to come on your own."

He walked past me and out the door. I sighed, but it wasn't a sigh of relief. A growing sense of fear welled up inside of me like I've never felt before.

CHAPTER 57

LOGAN

I OPENED MY EYES to see a banana dangling above my face. I swatted it away and sat up.

"Look what I have!" Maddie was almost jumping with joy.

"How'd you get that down?" I want to eat it so bad.

"I threw a rock and actually hit a banana!" She inspected it. "How are we supposed to open this?"

I took it from her and looked it over. "Maybe we should chop it in half."

"Okay, sounds good to me."

I set it on the ground and raised my hand and brought it down on the banana. The ends split open and a mushy substance flew out.

"I don't think that's how you are supposed to open it."

"Obviously. Let's try to get another banana down." We threw multiple rocks up and after a few tries I hit one and it flew down. I caught it and looked it over again. "Maybe we have to break this big stem." I yanked on the stem but it wouldn't open. My left hand was on the bottom of the banana and pinching it. All of a sudden the bottom tore open and the peel split. "I got it!"

I peeled the rest of the banana and broke off a piece for Maddie. "One, two, three!" We both took a bite of it and chewed. "It tastes... mushy, squishy. And it's sort of sweet, but not in a sugary way. It's good! It's like thick apple sauce... that's banana flavored."

Maddie shoved the rest of her banana in her mouth so she couldn't talk right. "Mhm!" Was all she could get out. She was laughing but it sounded all wrong because of the banana in her mouth and it made me burst out laughing at her.

We threw rocks up at the tree until we each knocked down a fair amount of fruit – including bananas. We put them in the bucket – it came in handy after all – and we started walking. We wanted to find a water source.

It didn't take long. We didn't see any more sources of food, but only a few minutes after we left the fruit tree we found a lake. It wasn't huge, but it was a few miles wide. I dropped the bucket on the ground and Maddie and I both sprinted towards the water. We jumped in and dove under the water. It felt amazing. I rubbed water all over and scraped off at least ten layers of dirt, dust, grime, and skin from my arms, legs, and chest. Maddie did the same to her arms and legs.

We stayed for hours swimming and cleaning and just relaxing in the water.

"I don't think I've ever enjoyed water more than I do right now," Maddie said.

"Same here."

We settled down on the bank to dry off. It was getting late and I was tired. I almost fell asleep, but all of a sudden water rained down on me. I jerked and opened my eyes. Maddie was ringing out her hair over my face. I jumped up and picked her up. She kicked her legs and wrapped her arms around my neck.

"Aaah!" She was screaming.

I walked towards the water and when I reached it I paused. I acted like I was going to set her down and she calmed a little. Then with all my strength I swung her out over the water and dropped her.

Splash!

She came up and wiped her eyes. She opened them and looked at me, and I knew that those eyes were happy.

CHAPTER 57

ANA

"WE'RE FROM KENTUCKY," Molly said. "We've been traveling with this caravan for a few months now –"

"Ana!" I heard. I turned around and saw Carter sprinting at me. We all stopped and waited for Carter to reach us. He was out of breath and his face was red. His eyes were filled with terror.

"What, Carter?" I asked.

He leaned on his knees and tried to control his breathing. "York!" He wheezed.

"York? What about him?"

"Who's York?" Marcus said.

I held up my hand at Marcus. "Hold on."

"What is going on, Carter? You're scaring me!"

He stood up, his breathing under control, and said, "He's here, Ana. York is here somewhere! I saw him last night coming back to the room; only I didn't know it was him. It was too dark to recognize him and he had shaved. And just now, I went back to the cart and he was in the room! He was there waiting for us!"

My jaw dropped. My heart beat increased and I had to close my eyes and try to calm down so I could think. "We have to get away before he sees us Carter!" I whispered.

"It's too late for that. He saw you with Marcus yesterday and he saw me watching. He knows we are here and he's coming for us. Only he said he wants us to choose to come with him. He doesn't want to force us to go with him."

"Like that's ever going to happen! I'm never going to go with that monster!" I exclaimed.

"I'm sure he will find a way to prove you wrong."

"Who is this guy? Where does he want to take you?" Marcus asked. Matt and Molly had wandered away when Carter interrupted Molly. Carter and I explained to Marcus how York had kidnapped us and wanted us to be slaves or something. He had some reason to put us to work. Marcus listened intently and after we were finished he was stunned. "Well, what does he look like?" Marcus asked. We described him and Marcus said, "We have to keep on the lookout. Don't drop your guard ever. I think we've forgotten, being in this little paradise, what it's really like out there. We don't trust anyone. Only ourselves. I figured that out from the moment I met you two."

I said, "That's because you were trying to steal Carter's backpack!" I joked, surprising myself that I still had a sense of humor.

He held up his hands in defense. "I was just looking to see if you had anything good in there… which you did. But, you caught me before I could steal anything. And I turned out to be a pretty great guy, am I right?" He wiggled his eye brows and winked at me.

I rolled my eyes and turned my attention back to Carter. I pushed away the joking manner that had come upon us and turned the conversation in a more serious direction. "We have to be ready. We have to go back to our room and figure out a plan before York does."

We decided to just keep our guard up and to stay together at all times. We were going to keep to ourselves and stay alert.

There was no sign of York. We packed out bags, were prepared to leave at any moment. No matter where we went, who we talked to, we were covering our tracks, constantly checking behind us, unable to rid the feeling of paranoia. But after a few days and not even a sighting of York, Marcus and I started to wonder. I felt bad, but I asked Carter anyways. "Are you sure it was really York that you saw?"

He looked at me in disbelief. "Of course it was York! Why would I make something like that up?"

"Are you sure it wasn't just someone who looked like York?"

"Ana, I can't believe you are even asking me this! I know for sure that it was York! He talked to me. He is here, Ana."

"Okay, okay. Calm down. I'm not trying to upset you —"

"Really? Because it seems as if you are!" Carter begins to raise his voice.

"I'm not. I think I'm just paranoid because York is here. I'm sorry, Carter."

"It's okay."

"Let's go walk somewhere. Down by the water, just the two of us."

"Isn't that breaking one of the rules?" he asked me.

"Yeah, but I think a few minutes is going to be okay. Come on, Carter, let's go."

We sauntered down to the water and walked along the shore. It was quiet and peaceful and just the two of us. We didn't need to talk. It was just nice to feel relaxed and calm. We sat down because Carter wasn't feeling too well. Once the last van in the caravan passed us, we stood up and continued walking. We didn't want to fall too far behind.

There was a splash in the water behind us. We stopped and turned around. Standing in the water was York. I gasped and he walked towards us. We started to pick up our pace and jogged towards the caravan.

"Hold up," York yelled. We didn't slow. "I said, hold up!" Again, we didn't slow. All of a sudden Marcus stepped out of the caravan before us.

"Marcus, go! York is here!" I yelled. He didn't budge. We reached him and stopped. "Come on, Marcus." I grabbed his arm and turn him around, but when I started to walk, Marcus pulled me back. "Marcus, what are you doing?"

"Hi, son," York said.

"Hi, Pop."

CHAPTER 59

CARTER

"Pop?" Ana questioned in disbelief.

I was furious. "Here's a pop for you!" I swung my arm and popped Marcus squarely in the nose. Marcus became furious and was about to hit me back but York interfered.

"Don't son. We need them strong and not broken."

Marcus stepped back and stared at us. His anger was replaced by a look of sorrow and almost shame. "Marcus..." Ana started. "How? How could you do this to us? I thought we were a team."

York replied for Marcus. "It was a quiet simple plan you see. There was no doubt in my mind that you two would try to escape from me. Which by the way, I need my VCRs back. Anyways, before I contacted you two on the VCRs I had called my son. He was in Ohio still and had agreed to search for you two. When he found Carter's backpack and such things on the ground, he called me from his VCR. Only, he wasn't sure whose things they were. I told him to look through the backpack and see if my two VCRs were in there. Naturally they weren't, but I made him double check.

"Then you two arrived at the scene. Carter was wounded making it very sad and dramatic, believe me, it really broke my heart," York covered his heart with mock sympathy on his face. "But nevertheless I knew it was you. Marcus had his VCR turned on so I could see for sure that it was you two. Then you sent him into the woods to get firewood. Which he did, but he also talked to me and we set up a plan.

"You traveled together, and laughed together… You three trusted one another. If only you had listened to Ana and not let your guard down, maybe you wouldn't be in this mess. Either way, I was very upset to find out that my son had taken a liking to a pretty, young girl named Ana. I was afraid the plan wouldn't be continued so I came down in search of you for myself. Although I trust my son, I trust myself more to get the job done."

York continued, "So, now here we are. A big happy family? I don't think so. We can be though, if you choose to come with Marcus and me willingly. You only have to say three little words. 'I will come.' That can't be so hard now, can it?"

York stopped talking, folded his hands, and stared at us. I was welling up with anger. "There is no way I am going with you," I spat at York.

"Marcus," York said, "go ahead."

All of a sudden Marcus grabbed Ana and threw her over his shoulder. Ana started to scream for help, but by now the caravan was gone. We were forgotten. Marcus trudged over to York and set Ana on the ground. He tied her hands behind her back and held a knife to her throat.

"Let her go!" I yelled.

"We will let her go, Carter," York said. "All you have to do is come with us. Ana is ready to go. Don't you want to save her, lover boy?" Marcus and York started to walk backwards towards the wall of the canyon. I stepped forward. York leaned into Marcus and whispered something I couldn't hear. Then Marcus pushed Ana ahead of him and the crossed the stream.

They continued walking until they reached the side of the canyon, and Marcus untied Ana's hands. He yelled something at her and she started to climb. I turned my attention back to York. "Why are you doing this? Why are we so important?"

"You don't understand, boy. Do you know how many strong, healthy, hard-working people are out there? Not many! I have to find some young teens to work because adults are too lazy to do it! I need to find people who have many good, strong years left in them and won't die off too quickly. You and Ana are perfect. That's why I need you."

I looked over at Ana and saw her and Marcus climbing up, getting closer to the top with every step. I looked back at York and saw he was just standing before me, watching Marcus and Ana. I made the decision fast, with no thought behind it, and I dashed into the stream. I tried to sprint through the water, but the current picked up speed making it difficult. I made it to the other side though, and could see York is pursuing me.

Once I was out of the water I picked up my pace and sprinted to the canyon wall. Before I climbed up I turned to see how far away from York I was. He was stepping out of the stream. I knew that because I was still regaining my strength he would be on me in a second, but I knew I had to try anyway. But then there was a thud and a splash. York turned around.

Directly behind him in the water was the beast.

CHAPTER 60

ANA

MARCUS WAS YELLING at me to walk faster. I was trying, but I was afraid of heights. There were pebbles and stones all over. I didn't want to step on a loose rock and fall. We were half way to the top of the canyon, and we stopped on a ledge that expanded away from the canyon wall about six feet. We looked over the side and we could see down into an alcove in the canyon was a pool of water. I couldn't tell how deep it was, but it was pretty big.

All of a sudden I heard a thud and a splash. I turned my gaze to Carter and found him at the bottom of the canyon. He started climbing up through the rocks and gravel. York was at the water and behind York was a creature. It was enormous. Black fur and bright red eyes. It could only be one thing. The beast.

It took a mighty leap over York and landed on the other side of the stream. It turned around to face York and it stared at him, growling. Its nostrils flared as it breathed in an out, steam blowing out of its nose. Marcus dashed away from me. He had forgotten me in his desperate attempt to run away, but on his way out he stepped on the edge of the ledge. Parts of the rock broke off and Marcus almost fell. He jumped and landed on the other side. On the main wall of the canyon.

He continued to make his way up the side of the mountain forgetting me, Carter, and his dad. *What a baby.*

All I knew was that when some of the rock started to crumble away, it left cracks on the ledge. I picked up a rock and threw it. It landed on the crack and broke it. The rocks fell down fifty feet and rolled to the edge of the pool of water. I was stuck. The hole between me and the main canyon wall is at least seven feet. *How am I going to get across that?*

There was a roar and I looked back at the beast. It was turning away from York who was left unharmed and it was stalking towards the canyon wall. He had found a new prey. I looked down and saw Carter scrambling up the unclean path trying to reach me.

"Carter, hurry!" I screamed. Carter looked back at the beast nearing him and continued to maneuver his way through the rocks. The beast took one leap and landed right behind Carter. "No!" I screamed. The beast opened his mouth revealing its sharp, dagger-like set of teeth and it lunged for Carter.

Carter tripped and stumbled to the side, just barely missing the beast's teeth. The beast lunged again and grabbed Carter by the shoulder. It carried Carter in his mouth and climbed up the canyon. It reached the top easily and set Carter on the ground. Carter's shirt was turning red from the wound in his shoulder, but he took no notice.

The beast turned around and jumped down the canyon. It stopped when it got to me. The beast stared me down, its menacing red eyes pierce through me causing my chest to tighten with fear. I could hardly breathe. That seven foot hole was nothing for the beast if it wanted me.

"Ana! Get out of there!" screamed Carter.

I wanted to look up at him, but I couldn't take my eyes off the beast. And, where was I supposed to go? The beast leaned back in a pounce position.

"Ana! The pool! Jump into the pool!"

I could just barely hear Carter. I stepped backwards until I could feel the edge of the ledge with my heel, never taking my eyes off the beast. For a quick second I looked down at the pool then returned my gaze to the beast.

In one instant that seemed to take place in slow motion, the world stopped. It was taciturn. The beast growled and leapt at me. He soared through the air at me, the wind rippling its thick fur. I heard Carter in the background shouting something incomprehensible. I turned on my heels, closed my eyes, and took a deep breath.

And I jumped.

CHAPTER 61

ANA

THUD! I SMACKED into something metal and hard. The wind was knocked out of me. There was no way I fell fifty feet, and no way had I landed in a pool. The wind was blowing my hair all over my face and whipping my clothes against me. I opened my eyes and looked down at a silver metal ship underneath me.

All of a sudden the floor dropped and I fell into the ship, hitting my head on the floor and then being consumed by darkness.

I opened my eyes and stared at a grey ceiling. The floor beneath me was cold and hard. As I slowly sat up my head pounded, the blood pushing against my ears and I became dizzy. I gently lowered myself back down on the floor and held my aching head. It was quiet around me except for the steady hum of an engine. *Where am I?*

After a few minutes I heard footsteps. I opened my eyes and Marcus was squatting on the ground before me.

"I see you're awake," he said.

"Marcus? What is going on?"

"I saved your life."

"So, you saved me from York?" I started. I became excited. "Where's Carter? Is the beast dead?" Marcus stopped me.

"I didn't save you from York, Carter isn't here, and I didn't see what happened to the beast after it landed in that pool. I'd assume it hit a rock and died, but you never know."

The realization sunk in. Marcus had me in a spaceship with him, Carter was somewhere with York, and the beast was probably still alive. And we didn't make it to Indianapolis. "Where are we going, Marcus?" I asked him.

"We are about to land and pick up my dad and Carter, and then we are heading to Washington D.C. Where do you think we are going?" He said with a mean tone to his voice.

The ship slowed and landed with a thud. A gust of wind blew in as the door opened and York stepped inside carrying Carter. Carter's hands were tied and he was unconscious. York spat, "It's about time you picked me up! I'd been waiting down there for five minutes trying to shut this boy up so I could tie up his wrists! I finally had to knock him upside the head so I could get a second of peace."

York dropped Carter with a *humph!* and looked at me. "I see you've decided to join the party. What a nice decision of you, to jump over the cliff right where Marcus was waiting for you. It's good to know that you follow orders."

At my confused gaze he continued. "Didn't Marcus tell you to jump? He left you there to run and get the ship and bring it around. You jumped at the perfect moment. I was watching. That beast, huh? Pretty amazing. Do you have any ideas where that thing came from?"

I heard a rustle on the ground and a faint whisper, "No…" Carter said, "Ana… no…." And then he was silent. I knelt on the ground beside him and tried to untie his wrists. The ropes wouldn't budge.

"York, please can't we untie him? He's already on the ship, knocked out, and there is nowhere for him to go."

York sighed. "Fine, Marcus toss me that knife." Marcus reached for a knife on the dashboard and tossed it to York. He caught it in mid-air, flipped it around, and before I realized what was going on Carter's hands were free. York had wicked skills with a knife. Just one more thing for me to watch out for.

"Let's go Marcus, start the engine and let's get this show on the road," York barked. Marcus started up the engine and the dashboard lit up displaying its intricate buttons, and we took off for Washington D.C.

END OF BOOK 1

ACKNOWLEDGEMENTS

First I would like to thank William Caulton because he put more faith in my writing than anyone and was the sole person I entrusted to read my story. For all of the encouragement and support you have given me I cannot thank you enough.

I would also like to thank my parents who have always supported me and encouraged me to follow my dreams and who taught me to work hard to accomplish them.

Hannah, because your music playlists played repeatedly during my writing and editing process.

Natalie and Laura, you have impacted my life in more ways than I can even count and your endless love has given me more strength than your will ever know.

Molly, you are a forever friend and such a treasure in my life. Thank you for always being there for me and for proving to me that distance doesn't always ruin relationships, but rather sometimes it makes them stronger.

Thank you to all my family and my friends who have always loved me and supported me.

Finally a very important thank you extends to my AuthorHouse staff who have guided me through this entire process. Without them my manuscript wouldn't be this beautiful book sitting in front of me.

About the Author

Katherine Helene is a writer, journalist and student. She adores the color yellow, vanilla pudding cups and her loveable kitty Garfield. She is excited to begin college at Grace College & Theological Seminary where she will study Journalism and Graphic Design, hoping to one day move to New York City where she can change the world one news report at a time.